LITTLE'S
LOSERS

Also by Robert Rayner
in the Lorimer Sports Stories series

Falling Star
Just for Kicks
Out of Sight
Suspended
Total Offence
Walker's Runners

LITTLE'S LOSERS

Robert Rayner

James Lorimer & Company Ltd., Publishers
Toronto

James Lorimer & Company Ltd., Publishers acknowledges the support of the Ontario Arts Council. We acknowledge the financial support of the Government of Canada through the Canada Book Fund for our publishing activities. We acknowledge the support of the Canada Council for the Arts which last year invested $20.1 million in writing and publishing throughout Canada. We acknowledge the Government of Ontario through the Ontario Media Development Corporation's Ontario Book Initiative.

The Canada Council | Le Conseil des Arts
for the Arts | du Canada

ONTARIO ARTS COUNCIL
CONSEIL DES ARTS DE L'ONTARIO

MIX
Paper from
responsible sources
FSC
www.fsc.org
FSC® C016245

Cover image: iStockphoto

Library and Archives Canada Cataloguing in Publication

Rayner, Robert, 1946-
    Little's losers / Robert Rayner.

(Sports stories)
Originally published under title: Miss Little's losers.
Issued also in electronic format.
ISBN 978-1-55277-839-5

    I. Title. II. Series: Sports stories (Toronto, Ont.)
PS8585.A974M58 2011   jC813'.6   C2011-903251-1

James Lorimer & Company Ltd.,
Publishers
317 Adelaide St. West
Suite 1002
Toronto, ON, Canada
M5V 1P9
www.lorimer.ca

Distributed in the United States by:
Orca Book Publishers
P.O. Box 468
Custer, WA USA
98240-0468

Printed and bound in Canada.
Manufactured by Friesens Corporation in Altona, Manitoba, Canada in July 2011.
Job # 66774

CONTENTS

1 Losers 7

2 Shay 18

3 Surprise Qualification 25

4 No Coach. Who Cares? 34

5 Miss Little's Losers 39

6 The *New* Brunswick Valley School Soccer Team 47

7 Lines, Patterns, Space — and Shay 59

8 Superstrike 64

9 You're Being Coached by Your *Kindergarten Teacher?* 73

10 Thrilled … and Scared 82

11 Dignity and Grace 92

12 The Magic Combination 103

1 LOSERS

You have to feel sorry for Shay, picking the ball out of the back of the net again. That's the eighth goal he's let in this afternoon. It must be pretty humiliating for a goalkeeper, letting in eight goals. No — make that nine goals. I always lose count after the first six. That means this season I've lost count in most of our games.

"Lo-sers. Lo-sers."

That's not a nice way to talk about a soccer team, is it? We're the losers, of course, and these are the supporters of the other team enjoying themselves by insulting us.

"Lo-sers. Lo-sers."

I think the game's nearly over. I hope so. I like playing, but it's getting late and I'm starving. I'm so hungry I might even eat the soccer ball next time it comes this way.

"Toby, help."

Do you suppose a soccer ball counts as a healthy snack? I'm trying to eat sensible foods that will help me lose weight.

"Toby, help!"

I wonder what's for supper. Scallops, with that brown rice Ma does — that'd be nice, if she can make it without turning the rice into a brown mush like she did last time.

"Toby, HELP!"

That sounds like Shay, our goalkeeper. I wonder what he wants.

"TOBY, HELP!"

"What's up, Shay?"

"You're playing soccer — remember? Look!"

He's pointing. Oh — right. I'm playing soccer, for our school, Brunswick Valley, against our old rivals St. Croix Middle School in the Southern New Brunswick Schools League. And here comes St. Croix, on the attack again. That's what Shay is pointing at. One of their forwards has the ball and is running down the wing... lipping easily past our midfielders... coming towards me. Here I go into the tackle. Oh — that's strange. I could have sworn he was in front of me, but somehow he's gotten behind me. Only Shay stands between him and the ball going into the net.

Correction: not *even* Shay stands between him and the ball going into the net.

"Sorry, Shay. I was daydreaming again."

"You're about as much use on defence as a piece of wood, Toby."

That's not Shay. That's Randy, the captain. He often

gets mad at us because we're so bad.

Goal number ten. Double figures again.

It's not that we play badly.

We play terribly.

We're awful.

We're so bad it's embarrassing.

I suppose I don't help the team much. I try, but this is my first season playing soccer, so I'm still learning. Perhaps I'm a bit old — I'm twelve and I'm in grade seven — to be learning a new sport. I've done cross-country running before, but that's a lot different from soccer. When I'm running, all I have to worry about is me. When I'm playing soccer, I have a whole team to worry about. My friend Shay is helping me. "Toby Morton," he says, "you've got to learn how to use the space on the soccer field better."

"Okay. Tell me about it," I say.

He says, "You open up space when one of our players has the ball, and close down space when one of their players has the ball. It's called the craft of making and controlling space. You've heard of handicraft and woodcraft and field craft, haven't you? Well, this is space craft."

During the next game, the other team was coming towards me with the ball and Shay called, "Toby, space craft!"

I thought he was talking about flying saucers and looked up expecting to see invading Martians. Then the ball hit me on the head and I fell over. That led to another goal.

I think one of the reasons I'm not good at space is that I'm not the fastest soccer player in the world. This might be because I'm a bit overweight. Not seriously overweight, and I'm getting slimmer by exercising and eating healthy foods, but I've still got a long way to go. The way Shay puts it, tactfully, is, "Toby, you're a bit on the chubby side." The only thing about me that looks athletic is my blond hair, which I have cropped close and spiky, like some of the soccer players I've seen in the sports magazines.

The other thing Shay keeps telling me is that I've got to stop daydreaming and concentrate on the game. I don't think there's much chance of that happening. It's one of the few things I do well, daydreaming. That, and running off at the mouth, usually with a few wisecracks thrown in.

It's alright to daydream when you're cross-country running. All you have to remember is to put one foot in front of the other and follow the trail. In fact when I'm running I like to daydream, usually about pizza, or fish and chips. But, like I said, in soccer you have to stay wide awake, because you've got the whole team, not to mention the other team, to worry about. On the other hand, the team — your team — is looking out for you, which feels nice.

Shay's good at looking out for others. That's how

we became friends. At my very first soccer practice the coach looked me up and down, sighed, and asked if I was sure I really wanted to play soccer. I nodded.

"Can you kick with both feet?" he asked. I said not at the same time because I'd fall over. He groaned, "I don't know where to put someone like you. You'd better try fullback."

When I got into position, I mumbled to myself, "What does he mean — someone like me?" Shay came over and said, "He means at fullback you need someone not super fast, but super *dependable*."

There's Shay kicking the ball upfield for the game to restart. Steve, our best striker — not that that's saying anything — is taking the kickoff at centre. He's passed to Randy, who's setting off toward the other side's goal. Steve is running forward, too. I suppose he's looking for space. Randy's passing the ball back to Steve, but the pass isn't a good one, and the ball's gone out of play. It's a throw-in for the other side.

St. Croix is known as an unscrupulous team. Our coach told us that, and I had to look up 'unscrupulous' to find out what he was talking about. It means they don't care what they have to do to win. In soccer, this means they trip and elbow and push and kick. You're not supposed to do these things. They're called fouls. Well — you can kick the *ball*, of course, but you're not supposed to kick the players on the other team.

St. Croix seems to get away with doing an awful

lot of fouling. Like that. Did you see their midfielder elbow Silas, one of our forwards, out of the way? That's a foul, but the referee didn't even flinch. Now they're coming toward our goal again.

"Toby ... "

"I'm awake, Shay. Don't worry."

This time I'm concentrating, thinking of closing down the space. Their centre has the ball and is heading straight down the middle of the field. I can see another St. Croix forward coming up the wing.

"You take the winger. I've got this one covered," says Shay.

I move out toward the wing, thinking of controlling the space on that side. Shay moves out from his goal line, blocking the other forward. He passes the ball to my forward. It lands just in front of him. He's approaching me slowly, keeping the ball close to his feet. I hold my ground, moving sideways so that he has to take it closer to the touch line and out of play. I won't tackle him, not unless I have to, to stop him breaking for the goal. I just need to close down his space and stop him from passing the ball across our goalmouth. I keep my eyes fixed on the ball. Suddenly, I'm flat on my stomach, my face in the mud. The other St. Croix player has run into me from behind. The referee should call a foul, but I guess St. Croix will get away with it again. I look up in time to see the forward I was covering race past me toward our goal. Shay rushes out and flings himself at the forward's feet, smothering the ball.

Shay stands, holding the ball. He surveys the field, crafting spaces, I guess. Randy shouts for the ball. Shay swings his foot and kicks upfield. The ball arcs high into an empty space on the right side. Randy puts his hands on his hips and watches it go out of play.

"Why don't you put it into orbit next time?" he sneers at poor Shay.

St. Croix take the throw-in. Steve rushes forwards and intercepts. He swerves around two St. Croix players and heads for their goal. Silas and Jason are with him. We might score if Steve passes, but he won't. He says he doesn't trust anyone else to play half-decently. He's probably right. There — he's lost it.

Silas is sniping at him again: "Why didn't you pass, dummy?"

"Because you'd have messed it up," says Steve.

"I suppose you call losing the ball *not* messing it up, do you?"

Julie, one of our midfielders, puts in, "I wish you two could play soccer as well as you bug one another."

We go on like this all the time. It's embarrassing.

The St. Croix goalkeeper is leaning against one of the goalposts. He hasn't touched the ball since I don't know when. He's chatting and laughing with some of the kids from his school who have come to watch.

No one from our school comes to watch us. That's about the only good thing about our games. It's bad enough losing every time without people gawking at us. Well, why would anyone come to watch us? They know the result before the game even begins. They know we'll play terribly, and they know we'll lose.

Even Shay's granddad, who always came to our games at the start of the season, has given up coming to watch us, although Shay says he asks about every game. Actually, I think Shay asked him not to come because he was embarrassed about letting in so many goals with him on the sidelines.

We've got the ball again. That's one of the twins, Jillian, with it. Oh. And that's Jillian without it. She's lost it. She's not even going to try to win it back. She's just standing there with her arms out, looking helpless. Her twin, Jessica, is telling her she's useless. That's how we are. When we're not messing up, we're insulting one another.

"TOBY! HELP!"

My cue. Excuse me.

Uh-oh.

Too late.

"Sorry, Shay. I was thinking about how badly we play."

Goal number eleven. The spectators from St. Croix Middle School who have come to watch are chanting again: "Lo-sers. Lo-sers." You can't blame them. St. Croix is top of the league and we're bottom. We've been there since the start of the season and that's where we'll finish. And not just bottom, but way bottom.

Humiliatingly bottom.

Embarrassingly bottom.

Heartbreakingly bottom.

Ignominiously bottom.

We've lost every single game. We haven't even managed a draw.

There's the final whistle. Thank you, Mr. Referee, for putting us out of our misery.

We troop off the field, to another chorus of "Losers. Lo-sers," from the St. Croix faithful. Steve and Silas are sniping at one another again.

"I wish you'd learn to pass," says Steve.

"I wish you'd learn to shoot straight," Silas retorts.

Shay puts in, "Arguing won't help us win."

Steve turns on Shay. "If you didn't let in so many goals maybe we'd have a chance of winning. You call yourself a goalkeeper..."

Shay just shrugs. He's looking at Julie, who's in a huddle with the twins. I hear Jessica say something about if the team was all girls it would do better. She's probably right.

Here comes our coach, Mr. Cunningham, the math teacher at Brunswick Valley. He'll have something to say. Correction: he'll have something to shout. He's short and stocky and has lots of black hair and bushy eyebrows that meet in the middle. He looks fierce but he's alright, really, except that he gets mad at us when we lose, which means he's mad at us all the time. He was quite a famous player in his day. There's a team picture in the teachers' room of the Montreal Cougars the year they won the Eastern Canadian League Championship, and you can see Mr. Cunningham there, in the second row, so it must be hard for him, trying to coach a hopeless team like us. He gets so mad we think one day he might have a heart attack.

"I want all of you to come here."

We gather around Mr. Cunningham.

"What's up, Mr. C?" I ask.

"What's up? You lost eleven to zero."

"It could have been worse," I say.

Mr. Cunningham glares at me, his hands on his hips. "How could it have been worse, Toby?"

"It could have been twelve to zero, or thirteen to zero, or twenty to zero, or thirty to zero, or —"

"That's enough, Toby. It's nothing to make wisecracks about. Do you people understand just how bad you are? There are six teams in the league and you're sixth."

"That could be worse, too, Mr. C.," I say.

Mr. Cunningham still has his hands on his hips, and he's glaring at me so hard his eyes have gone narrow. "I don't want to hear about it."

I keep talking anyway, trying to cheer everyone up. "It would be worse if there were twenty teams in the league because then we'd be twentieth."

Mr. Cunningham snaps, "If there were one hundred

teams in the league I'm sure you'd manage to be number one hundred. I can't think of one good thing to say."

"I can," I say quickly. "We won't be in the playoffs."

Mr. Cunningham is shouting now. "What's good about that?"

"We won't lose any more games."

Mr. Cunningham is gasping for air. He's gone bright red. But he doesn't have a heart attack. Instead, he explodes. I don't mean literally, with little bits of him flying all over the field. I mean he goes nuts, verbally.

"I'm sick and tired of listening to your wisecracks, Toby. And I'm sick and tired of watching all of you play — *try* to play — soccer. You're hopeless. You're not just hopeless, you're beyond help. Not only are you awful soccer players, but on top of that you're nasty and rude to one another, and all you can do is joke about it. I've had it. I quit."

2 SHAY

We're walking home, Shay and me, when Shay says, "What am I going to tell Granddad?"

"What do you mean?" I say.

But I know what he means. He means he's afraid his granddad will be disappointed in him, letting in all those goals, and us losing again. I feel sorry for Shay — not that his granddad's unkind to him or anything — but the old fellow used to be quite a famous goalkeeper. That would be in the old days, mind you, about a hundred years ago. He's an old guy now. I think Shay said he turned sixty this year. So of course Shay feels he ought to be a good goalkeeper too, and that means not letting so many goals in. Good luck, with players like me on defence.

Speaking of families, don't even mention Steve's old man. One time Steve's dad came to watch, and of course Steve didn't score any goals and he went ballistic right in front of us. He's an important businessman — owns Maritime Aquaculture Enterprises — and his company was going to buy us new uniforms. Until he

18

saw us, that is. After watching us lose 12–0 to Keswick Narrows, he told Mr. Cunningham he didn't want his company associated with a bunch of incompetent nincompoops like us (that's what he called us, really he did). You have to pity poor Steve. His dad expects him to be this awesome soccer player and to score lots of goals. Steve's always making excuses for the way he acts, saying he has high expectations and stuff like that.

I guess none of that matters now, with us finished for the season, and probably finished for good, with no one to coach us.

"I wish I was a good goalkeeper," Shay says.

"You are a good goalkeeper," I shoot back. "It's not your fault you let in goals with a slug like me as a defender. Remember that great save you made when I got pushed over?"

"But I let in at least three goals I should have saved. Like that first goal ... "

"Anyone can drop the ball, Shay."

"Goalkeepers can't — and they certainly can't drop the ball in front of the other side's centre and then stand there looking at him while he says 'thank you' and kicks it into the net."

That really happened. Poor Shay.

"And that goal I let in when Jillian had the throw-in at our end and she tried to throw to me."

"It wasn't your fault the ball went over your head and into the net."

"Did you hear the St. Croix players laugh?"

Like I said — poor Shay.

I try to cheer him up. I tell him about a goalkeeper I once knew (I didn't really; I was just making this up) who let in so many goals he decided to kill himself. "So he goes to the railroad tracks and waits until he hears a train. Then he jumps on the tracks, and the train's coming straight towards him."

I knew Shay would fall for it.

"What happened?" he asks.

"It went right through his legs," I say.

"So he wasn't hurt, then?" Shay says.

Poor Shay.

We leave the bright lights of Main Street — that'd be the lights in the Main Street Convenience — and turn onto the street we both live on. It's called Riverside Drive, but the river is way over behind a mess of alders and bog, and it actually bends away from the street, so Riverside Drive isn't beside the river at all. I don't know why they call it that. But it makes about as much sense as Main Street being called Main Street when Brunswick Valley has only two other roads to compare it to. It'd make more sense to call it Just About The Only Street.

We arrive at Shay's house, where his granddad runs a flower shop out of the converted garage. A sign over the door says "Sutton's Flowers." The flower shop delivery van is parked in the driveway.

"Granddad's probably in the shop," says Shay.

As soon as we open the door, the smell of hundreds of flowers hits us like a summer rain shower. Although it's fall, I feel as if it's midsummer. I expect to see birds and butterflies flitting around. The shop is so packed with flowers of different sorts and sizes you have to weave through them to cross it. At one end is a small counter cluttered with papers and dried flower arrangements. Shay's granddad, Mr. Sutton, is behind it, arranging bunches of flowers.

"Hello, boys," he says. "How did the game go?"

I look at Shay. His head is down and he doesn't answer.

"We lost, but Shay played really well in goal," I say. I think of the amazing save he made when he threw himself at the St. Croix forward's feet and say, "He made a brilliant save. He made lots of brilliant saves."

"How did you play, Toby?" Mr. Sutton pokes me in the stomach. He's always making little jokes about me being chubby — not mean jokes, but nice, kind ones, meant to make me keep on losing weight. "I expect you gave a ... " he chuckles " ... a *stout* performance."

He laughs so much at his own joke that he has to sit down. I laugh, too. Shay just looks at us like we're crazy.

When he's recovered, Mr. Sutton says, "Never mind losing, boys. Someone always has to lose, and the important thing is to enjoy playing, and to play your best. Did you play your best?"

I look at Shay. His head is hanging again.

"I guess so," I say.

Mr. Sutton says, "How about you, Shay?"

"I let in eleven goals," he says bitterly.

Mr. Sutton puts down the bunch of flowers he's holding and squeezes Shay's shoulder. "I once let in *twelve* goals," he says. "It was in Winnipeg in — let's see — 1970. It was in the old Pan-Canadian League, and I was in goal for the Maritime Athletics. We were playing the Winnipeg Blizzard. It was in a near blizzard, too, I remember. It was snowing heavily when the game started, and by halftime I could hardly see the ball. The first goal came after only two minutes, when one of our midfielders lost control of the ball and missed … "

He sits down again, lost in the memory. Shay sits too, with his elbows resting on the shop counter and his chin in his hands, watching his granddad. I look from one to the other. They're a sturdy pair, not tall, but solid. I've seen Mr. Sutton in shorts and you should see the muscles in his legs. His hair is like a white mop, and he has a round, smiley face, with white eyebrows and sparkly eyes. Shay's hair is the same, except it's black, not white, and he has a round face, too. But it's not as smiley as his granddad's, and Shay's eyes don't sparkle as much. Mr. Sutton is still reminiscing about his days as a goalkeeper in England and in Canada. He's always reminiscing about soccer. He goes on for ages. It's quite interesting, usually, and I like to listen to him, but if I don't have something to eat soon I'll collapse.

I whisper, "I have to get home," and tiptoe out. Mr. Sutton waves, and Shay mouths, "See you tomorrow."

I go a bit further up Riverside Drive to my house. Some of the houses — the ones as far along the Drive as Shay's — have little gardens and bushes and lawns. Shay's granddad has all sorts of flowers growing by the path leading to his shop, just like you'd expect. But the further up the Drive you go, the less vegetation you see. It's mostly dirt, and if there's any colour at all, it comes from the few mangy trees, or more likely from old trucks rusting in yards. It's not hard to pick out my house. It's the one with the mangy trees *and* the dirt *and* the old truck. Some of the other houses have trucks, and some have dirt, and some have mangy trees — but only my house has *all* of them. I like the old truck in the yard. It won't win us a prize in the Brunswick Valley Best-Kept Garden competition, but I'm used to having it around.

My stepdad, Conrad, is in the yard raking leaves. I suddenly remember I was supposed to help him, but he doesn't say anything. Conrad likes raking leaves. He likes doing anything energetic. He has the sleeves of his flannel shirt rolled up, showing off his brawny arms, his Flames baseball cap pulled down over his thick black hair. Conrad's big and solid. Ma's big too, but she's not solid. In fact, she's what Conrad calls fleshy. Her tummy and her arms and her legs jiggle when she walks. She keeps saying she's going to eat healthier foods and get her weight down, like I've been trying to do, but each time she starts it doesn't last long.

Conrad stops raking and slowly smiles when he sees me. His grey eyes crinkle. "How'd the game go today, big guy?" he says.

"We lost again," I reply.

"You should call yourselves the Brunswick Valley Maple Leafs," he chuckles, and slaps me on the back.

At least my ma and stepdad don't have high expectations of me in soccer, like Shay's granddad and Steve's dad. Ma says, "That's nice, lovey," whatever happens.

I go inside. Ma's in the kitchen getting supper ready.

"We lost again, Ma," I declare.

"That's nice, lovey."

"We lost eleven to zero, Ma."

"That's nice, lovey."

I know she's not listening.

"We lost fifty to zero, Ma."

"That's nice, lovey."

"We lost a hundred to zero, and all the rest of the team got eaten by crocodiles, Ma."

"That's nice, lovey. Here's your supper."

3 SURPRISE QUALIFICATION

At assembly the next Monday morning, I'm daydreaming, as usual, while Shay, beside me, is sneaking glances at Julie.

I'm daydreaming about this movie I watched over the weekend called *Space Rebels*, about this group of kids whose parents get captured by aliens who are taking over Earth. The aliens don't bother to capture the children because they think they can't do anything to resist them. But the kids form a rebel group and fight the aliens. They lose in the end, but I liked it anyway. Although they lost, they never gave up, and everyone, even the aliens, respected them for trying.

When I started my daydream, Mr. Walker, the principal, was going on — and on — about how our little Brunswick Valley School was a family, and how all the students, from kindergarten to grade eight, were part of that school family, so all of us should look out for the others, and especially for the little ones. It's nice of him to say this, but he doesn't really need to because we usually do it anyway. After all, with only about two hundred and fifty kids in the school, we know one another pretty well.

Then something Mr. Walker says — about how one part of the Brunswick Valley School family is the soccer team — grabs my attention, so I tune out the space rebels and tune in the principal.

"The team did not have one of their ... " Mr. Walker sort of coughs, and goes on, "One of their better seasons, but despite this I'm pleased and proud to announce that they've made the provincial playoffs."

I can't believe I'm hearing this. Neither can Shay, who's managed to drag his eyes from Julie, and is gaping first at me and then at Mr. Walker.

"Did I hear that right?" I whisper to Shay.

Ms. Watkins, the French teacher, standing at the end of our row, says, "Toby, are you talking?"

That's got to be one of the stupidest questions teachers ask. First, what am I supposed to say? No — I'm catching flies? And second, if *I'm* not supposed to be talking, then it makes it twice as bad if *she* starts talking, because now two of us are breaking the rules, and three times as bad if I'm expected to answer, because then I've got to talk some more.

"No, Ms. Watkins," I say. "I'm catching flies."

"I'll see you at recess, Toby."

"It'll be my pleasure, Ms. Watkins," I say, and turn my attention back to Mr. Walker.

"…and the soccer team's first game will be against Keswick Narrows Memorial on Wednesday, at Keswick Narrows."

I look at Steve and Randy and Silas. They can't believe what Mr. Walker is saying, either. They're shaking their heads and frowning. Randy is tapping his head, suggesting that Mr. Walker is going crazy.

"I'd like to compliment our soccer team on their fine effort at reaching the provincials…" the principal goes on.

Everyone in the school knows we lost every game. I can hear students giggling at how ridiculous it is for us to be in the playoffs. They've been making up jokes about us all season. One of the more common ones is: "What do you call a Brunswick Valley soccer player with half a brain?" and someone answers, "A *gifted* soccer player." Or how about: "Why do the Brunswick Valley soccer players carry lighters?" and the answer is, "Because they always lose their matches." We've been more popular than knock-knock jokes this year.

Mr. Walker finishes, "…and I'd like to ask the soccer team to stand and be recognized."

He must be joking. There's no way I'm standing. It's embarrassing enough just sitting here with my head down while everyone is laughing at us. But before I can stop him, Shay promptly stands. Everyone is looking around, grinning and snickering, waiting to see the worst soccer team in the world. But all they see is Shay.

The others, like me, wish they were invisible. Some of the younger kids start clapping, but they're soon drowned out by the howls of laughter. One group of grade seven students is chanting, in a whisper, "Lo-sers. Lo-sers." Shay blushes and quickly sits down.

At recess, after Ms. Watkins has finished lecturing at me about talking in assembly, I go looking for Shay. I find him outside, watching a bunch of little kids playing dodge ball on the playground.

"What's up?" I say.

He doesn't answer. He's off in another world, the way he gets sometimes. He gets this glazed look in his eyes. I see it when we play soccer. It's not that he's not concentrating, like me. In fact, it's the opposite. He's concentrating hard on something I can't even see. It's as if he's in a secret soccer world of his own. I saw that look during the game against St. Croix, when he kicked the ball into the empty space and it rolled out of play — the time Randy got mad and made the crack about why didn't he just put the ball into orbit. I wonder whether Shay should have been mad at Randy and the others for not seeing the space the way he did.

Anyway, he's standing there with this faraway look in his eyes, and when he does speak his voice is far away.

"Look at the patterns those kids are making in that little space as they try and dodge the ball," he says.

"Like what?" I say.

"Those three girls — look — they're making a

triangle with equal sides."

"An equilateral triangle," I say, showing off. We learned this stuff with Mr. Cunningham in math class last year. I seem to remember Shay finding it dead easy, while the rest of us struggled.

"Now one of the girls has moved, and that's turned it into an isosceles triangle," Shay goes on.

"Wha ... ?" I sputter.

"A triangle with two equal sides," Shay explains.

"So?"

"So it's changed the space around them. It's made space behind the girl who's moved. Now — look — it's gone scalene ... "

"Scalene?"

"Where none of the sides are the same." Shay adds dreamily, "That's the best kind of triangle for making space."

I don't know what he's talking about. All I see is a bunch of little kids running around while one hurls a ball at the legs of the others.

" ... Now another kid's there and — look — they're making a parallelogram ... "

At least I know that's a four-sided shape with the opposite sides equal and parallel.

" ... Watch what happens when two of them move in the same direction. There — they're stretching the parallelogram, and that makes space open at one end as they move."

I've lost him now. I wait for Shay to come back to Earth. He's still watching, seeing shapes and spaces and patterns I can't see. When I get tired of waiting, I say, "You're a space cadet."

"What?"

"Earth to Shay. Are you receiving me? Come in, Shay."

"What are you going on about?"

He's back. "I said you're a space cadet."

"Why?"

"Because you're always looking at spaces and shapes and patterns, and when you do, you get this funny, way-off look about you. Are you back on Earth now?"

"Funny."

"Because if you are, there's something we've got to do."

"What's that?"

"We've got to find out what Mr. Walker was talking about in assembly, about us being in the playoffs. It doesn't make sense. You don't lose every game and then make it to the playoffs. Besides, do you *want* to get beaten again — this time in the playoffs?"

"We haven't got a coach anyway. Mr. Cunningham got angry with us and said he was quitting, remember?"

"Right. So let's find out what's going on."

We set off for Mr. Walker's office, talking about the provincial playoffs along the way. They're these games at the end of the regular season when the top teams from all the school leagues in the province are drawn to play each other in regional round-robin tournaments. Then the winners of the round-robin tournaments have a playoff to see who gets to represent each area of the province — southern, northern, central, and city. That's when things get tough. Whichever team gets to represent southern New Brunswick — it's never us, of course — usually gets blown away at the next stage, and if you draw one of the big city schools, you're in for a whipping.

We find Steve outside Mr. Walker's office. He's on the same mission as we are. Mr. Walker's door is closed and we can hear voices coming from inside. At first they're sort of muffled and we can't make them out — not that we're trying to — but then someone booms, "No. No way. I've had it with them."

It's Mr. Cunningham. He's almost shouting, just like he does when he's coaching us. Correction: when he used to coach us.

We look at one another, embarrassed, wondering whether we should just creep away, when the door opens and we hear Mr. Walker say, "Please, Mr. Cunningham — Jeff — reconsider your decision. The kids deserve the chance to play."

Mr. Cunningham hasn't seen us yet. He's glaring back into the office at Mr. Walker. "No. That's final. I told the soccer team I was done with coaching them and I'm not changing my mind. They can't play soccer and their attitudes stink. They're just a bunch of hopeless losers."

He turns to go and sees us waiting in the hallway. We're frozen with embarrassment. Mr. Cunningham glares at us, snorts like a moose, and stomps off down the hallway.

"Let's leave," Shay mutters.

Steve and I nod in agreement, but before we can sneak away Mr. Walker emerges, looking after Mr. Cunningham and shaking his head. He sees us and asks, "What is it, guys?" He sounds tired.

"It doesn't matter," Shay says quickly.

We're shocked that Mr. Cunningham is so down on us. I knew we were bad, but ... *that* bad?

"It can wait," Steve mumbles.

I just nod.

"You came to ask me about something, and I'd guess it's about soccer, since you're all on the soccer team. Am I right?"

We nod, still too embarrassed and shocked to speak. Finally Steve blurts out, "How come we're in the play-offs when we didn't win a single game and we finished bottom of the league?"

"I thought that might be it," says Mr. Walker. "This is what happened. Two teams had to drop out, one because the school couldn't afford a bus to get them to the playoffs, and the other because five members of the team were caught drinking at a school dance ... " Steve whistles in surprise, and Mr. Walker repeats, "Yes — five. Stupid, eh? Anyway, according to their school policy that means automatic suspension from all sports activities. Now they can't get a team together. That means you qualify, despite your — er — your difficulties this season."

"You mean despite the fact that we stink," I say.

"No," says Mr. Walker, gently. "I mean, you've had your difficulties this season."

"But if we're in the playoffs — who will coach us?" Shay asks timidly.

Mr. Walker shakes his head. "I got the call about the playoffs just before this morning's assembly. I didn't know Mr. Cunningham had resigned when I made the announcement. In fact, I didn't know until just now. I don't know who will coach you."

"It doesn't matter," Steve says. "There's no point in playing. We're no good. We'd only lose again."

"Don't be too hard on yourself," Mr. Walker chides. "It's always worth trying again. And you must care some, or you wouldn't be here now. Right?"

Steve shrugs.

Shay nods.

"We have nowhere to go but up," I say.

"I'd coach you myself but I just don't have time now," the principal adds, "and I have to be away at meetings through much of the playoffs. That wouldn't be fair to the team. But let me think about it. Come and see me tomorrow."

4 NO COACH. WHO CARES?

We know the news isn't going to be good the next day before Mr. Walker even speaks. He shakes his head as soon as he sees us peer around the door of his office.

Mr. Walker's not huge, but he's wiry and athletic, and he's always moving — pacing, or bouncing up and down, or swinging his arms. He has this craggy face, and long hair that he ties back in a ponytail. We think he's cool, but we'd never tell him that. His office is about the size of a closet, so with the four of us in there — athletic, bouncy Mr. Walker, solid Shay, gangly Steve, and chunky me — there's hardly room to breathe. It may be small, and it's painted the usual boring school yellow, like the hallways, but he's tried to make his closet welcoming to us kids, with movie posters on the walls and books on a little table.

Once we've all squeezed in, Mr. Walker begins: "No luck finding a coach for you, I'm afraid. I went to all the teachers and asked if they would coach the soccer team, just through the playoffs, and either they're too busy or they say they don't know enough about soccer, or they say they don't see any point in working with a team that has such a poor record — and, I'm sorry to say, such a bad attitude." He pauses and adds, "Is that being unfair?"

We hang our heads. We know it's true, about the attitude.

"We kept losing, and then we got mad at one another because nothing would go right," I offer. I sound pathetic.

"I'm really sorry, guys. I tried," Mr. Walker concludes, shepherding us out.

We mutter, "Thanks anyway, Mr. W."

"Who cares about the playoffs anyway?" I say as we amble down the hallway.

I'm trying to cheer them up, but at the same time I'm asking myself — why *should* we care? A few days ago we were glad the season had ended for us, and now we're trying to find a coach so we can keep playing. It doesn't make sense.

"That's what I thought — who cares about the playoffs?" Shay says, "until Mr. Walker said we were in them. Then I started to think — it would be nice to have one more chance to play half-decently, even if we lose. I feel sort of... sort of ashamed — not just because we lost all those games, but because we were mean to one another."

Shay is seriously upset. The kids were always on

his case about him letting in so many goals, although many of them weren't his fault, and while we were all mean to one another, he got the worst of it. And now *he's* the one feeling ashamed? I feel like apologizing to Shay for all the times I let him down, and all the times the other kids insulted him. Steve's hanging his head, knowing he was about the worst for getting on Shay. He really should apologize to Shay, but he does something even better.

He agrees with him.

"You're right. I feel the same," he says, slowly looking up at Shay. "At first I thought I never want to play soccer again, but then I thought — I'd like one more chance to show we're not so hopeless."

Shay grabs his soccer ball from his locker. It's lunchtime so we've still got twenty minutes of break left. We go down to the field behind the school and start kicking the ball around.

I'm disappointed too, more for Shay and Steve than for myself. They deserve a better end to their season than being beaten 11–0 by St. Croix. They know something about soccer. They look like soccer players. Steve is tall, with gangly arms and legs. He has this mud-coloured hair that hangs down over his eyes like a horse's, until he runs, when it flies all around. Come to think of it, he looks a bit like a horse — not his face, but because of the way he moves, his legs pounding, leaving people behind easily. Shay, without ever seeming to hurry, collects the passes we send him and smoothly returns them. He seems better at collecting and sending passes than he is in goal. We're getting warmed up now, kicking the ball harder and further.

"Stretch the triangle. Make space," Shay calls.

There he goes again, talking about space and shapes and patterns. I don't understand, but Steve seems to.

Miss Little, the kindergarten teacher, is on yard duty. She stops to watch us. Shay gives a little wave, and she smiles and waves back, wiggling her fingers. The year we started school there was only one kindergarten, so we were all in Miss Little's class. Some years there are enough kids for two kindergarten classes, or for one and a combined kindergarten and grade one, but usually there's just one. That means Miss Little has taught most of the kids in the school.

"Getting ready for the playoffs, children?" she calls.

Shay replies glumly, "We're not in the playoffs because we don't have a coach."

"Oh, you poor dears," Miss Little says. "Tell me what's happened."

Shay and I go over to Miss Little. Steve hangs back. I can tell by his sulky face he doesn't like it when Miss Little calls us "children" and "poor dears." I don't mind. In fact, secretly, I kind of like it.

Miss Little is tall and thin, with long blond hair, and with big, round glasses that keep slipping down her nose. In kindergarten we used to get hypnotized by them, wondering whether they'd fall right off the end of her nose. They never did. Just when we thought they were going to, she'd push them back. When she looks down at us with her big blue eyes, it's as if we're in kindergarten again.

"Now, boys, tell me what's happened," she repeats.

She listens carefully as we tell her about losing all our games, and about being mean to one another. We tell her about Mr. Cunningham quitting, and about none of the other teachers being able to coach us.

"I guess I don't blame them," I finish. "Who'd want to coach a bunch of losers like us?"

"When Mr. Walker asked me if I'd coach, I said I couldn't help because I didn't know anything about soccer. But I hate to see you poor children —"

"We're not *children*," Steve interrupts, scowling. I didn't think he was listening.

Miss Little just looks at him and continues, "I hate to see you poor children unable to play. Let me see what I can do."

When we go in at the end of the lunch recess, Shay nudges me and points to the soccer bulletin board in the main hallway. It was empty when we went out, but now there's a notice on it. It's printed in perfect lettering with different coloured markers, and is decorated with little pink soccer balls all round the edges. It says, *Team meeting after school today.*

5 MISS LITTLE'S LOSERS

The meeting after school is held in the old art room. It's called the old art room because we don't do art any more, not since the old art teacher — she was old, too, Mrs. Levesque, at least forty — not since she left and the school didn't replace her. All the rooms are old because Brunswick Valley School is old. From the outside it looks like a prison, all brick and little windows. The school yard where we have recess looks like an exercise yard for prisoners, except for the little kids' playground in the corner. But the inside of the school doesn't look so much like a prison because they've tried to make it cheery, with all the classrooms and hallways painted bright yellow, which is nice if you like bright yellow.

I peer in the door. There's no one from the soccer team there; just Miss Little, sitting at the front of the room, sorting through a pile of little kids' paintings. She looks up and sees me. "Sorry, Miss Little," I say, "I was looking for the soccer meeting."

"That's right, Toby, dear. It's here. Come in."

With her head down as she looks at the paintings, her glasses have slipped right to the tip of her nose. I think — yes! This time they're going to fall. But at the last second she pushes them back.

I go in and take a seat. Miss Little smiles at me. I smile back.

"Is anyone else coming?" she asks.

"Shay said he'll be here," I say.

Right on cue, Shay arrives. He says, "What's up."

I say, "Yo."

Shay taught me to say that. I never used to know what to say when kids said, "Hey," or, "What's up," so I didn't say anything, and they thought I was being un-friendly. Then Shay told me it didn't matter what I said back, because "hey" was just something to say. It was just a sort of greeting noise, and all I had to do was make a sort of greeting noise back.

We practised.

Shay said, "What's up."

I said, "La-la-la."

Shay said to try any noise but that one, and try again. "What's up," he said.

I said, "How-dee-doo."

Shay said that wouldn't do either, and to just say, "Yo."

So now I say "Yo," and it seems to work. I guess it's like when adults say, "How are you?" and "I'm fine." They don't really care how you are, and they're prob-ably not really fine. They're just making a greeting noise.

At the start of term, Ms. Watkins was going through the class list. When she came to my name she read out, "Toby Morton," and sort of sighed, and said, "How are you, Toby?" Instead of saying, "As well as can be expected considering we're back in school," I said, "Yo, Ms. Watkins." She seemed to like it.

Shay stops at the door, like me, when he sees Miss Little. I wave him in as Miss Little smiles and says, "Come in, Shay, dear."

Shay sits across from me. We look at each other and at Miss Little. She's gone back to looking through the kindergarten paintings. I feel as if we're in kindergarten again. I wonder whether we should get out the paints and do a picture for Miss Little, then be sure to clean up after ourselves.

Suddenly Shay blurts out what we've both been thinking. "Are you going to coach us?"

"Yes, dear, if you'd like me to," answers Miss Little.

I catch Shay's eye. We're thinking the same thing again. We both love Miss Little. All the students do, even Steve, although he pretends not to. We all love her as our old kindergarten teacher, and we all love her as a teacher who always remembers our names, and who always remembers things about us and asks about them, and is always smiley and nice, but ... soccer coach?

You see, soccer's quite a complicated game. There are the forwards, who are supposed to get the ball into the other side's net. And there are the backs, the defenders, who are supposed to stop the other side scoring. And then there are the midfielders, who sort of defend when they have to and attack when they can. In our case, us being the worst team in the world, we have forwards who can't score, backs who can't defend, and midfielders who can't do either.

I'm thinking — how can we tell Miss Little she's out of her depth, especially with the first playoff game only two days away?

Steve is standing just outside the door. I don't know how long he's been there, but it's long enough for him to hear Miss Little say she'll coach us.

"What do you know about soccer?" he scoffs.

Miss Little agrees: "Nothing — but there are some important things I know that might help the team play better."

"Like what, Miss Little?" I ask.

"Like — remembering some of our kindergarten rules might help."

We're mystified.

Miss Little asks, "Do you remember being in kindergarten?"

Shay and I smile and nod. Steve shrugs.

"Everything worked out well in kindergarten, didn't it, dears?"

Shay and I agree again. We loved being in Miss Little's class. Steve did too, but he's not going to say so.

"Well, children — I think we can make things work

42

out quite well on the soccer field, if we remember some of the rules we learned in kindergarten."

Steve snorts, "My dad expects me to play well. He won't like me having someone for a coach who doesn't know soccer, and he especially won't like me having a girl for a coach."

Miss Little stands up and pushes her glasses back. Shay and I look at one another. We're thinking — uh-oh. We remember that look from kindergarten. Miss Little was always nice — but you didn't want to mess with her.

"First, Steve, dear, I'm a woman, not a girl," says Miss Little. "Second, you and your father can have me for a coach or no one at all, because I'm all you're going to get. And third — don't ever be rude to your coach again, because if you do, you'll be off the team — starting right now unless you apologize."

Steve harrumphs and leaves. A few moments later, we see him hanging around just outside the door.

"Well, Steve, dear? Are you staying?" Miss Little calls to him.

"I suppose."

"Come in, then. And what do we have to say after we've been rude?"

"Sorry."

"Apology accepted. Now, children, let's get down to business."

She sits. I feel as though we should gather in a little group at her feet so she can read us a story, but we sit at the tables. Miss Little asks where the rest of the team is.

"They didn't want to come," says Steve. "They're still mad at finishing bottom of the league and losing so badly against St. Croix. And when rumour went around that it was you calling the team meeting — someone saw you putting the notice up — they said they wouldn't come because ... because ... "

"You can tell me, Steve, dear. It won't count as being rude."

" ... because they said you were nice but you didn't know soccer."

"Can you — any of you — persuade any of them to come back?"

"I think I can persuade the twins," I say. "They didn't come just because they thought no one else was coming. Then there's Silas and Jason and Nicholas — but I don't think they'll come back."

"They'll come if I tell them," Steve puts in. "Leave them to me."

"That makes — let me see — eight," says Miss Little. "How many do we need for a soccer team?"

Shay and I glance at one another. Steve snorts but turns it into a cough.

"Eleven, Miss Little," I say.

Miss Little looks up at the ceiling. She's doing her teacher routine of pretending to be deep in thought. "We have eight players, and we need eleven, so — how many more players do we need?"

"Three, Miss Little," Shay and I chorus, like she wants us to. If it was just me there, I would have answered seriously, but because there are three of us, we pretend we're goofing around talking like this.

Steve rolls his eyes but doesn't say anything.

"We need three more," Miss Little repeats. "Shay, can you get anyone? Who else was on the team? Wasn't Julie playing? Could you ask her?"

Shay turns red and gulps: "I guess."

Julie is in grade eight, a grade above us, and Shay thinks she's a goddess. He's scared to talk to her.

"That would make nine," I say. "But the others — they won't come back. There's no point in asking."

Steve and Shay nod agreement.

"Well — we'll start with nine," says Miss Little. "Make sure you get after everyone we talked about, and make sure they — and you — remember there'll be a practice tomorrow after school, and then there's the game on Thursday." She holds her hands under her chin and claps them three times and says, "I know this is going to be *fun* and *exciting* for all of us. Now — off you go, children."

Shay and I look at each other and grin at how Miss Little talks to us. It's okay as long as no one else hears. Steve rolls his eyes again, but doesn't dare say anything.

We're heading for the door when Miss Little calls out, "One more thing before you go, children. Who was captain?"

"Randy — and he says he's never going to play for the school again after that last game. There's no point in asking," says Steve.

"Very well," says Miss Little, coming over to us. "Steve, dear, I want you to be captain. That's a lot of responsibility, but I think you can handle it. How about it?"

Steve nods. "Okay, I guess."

"You don't sound too sure, dear," says Miss Little. "Are you worried about something?"

Steve looks at his feet.

I say for him, "He's worried about what his dad will say about you being our coach — right, Steve?"

Steve nods.

"We'll deal with that when we have to — *if* we have to," says Miss Little, and pats Steve on the head.

Steve cringes. "Jeez, Miss Little. I'm not one of your kindergarten kids, you know."

Miss Little smiles at us and says, "You'll all always be my kindergarten children. Off you go now. Early to bed tonight and tomorrow, remember, so that you're ready for the game."

"Do you suppose we'll be ready?" I ask nervously as we walk away.

"Ready to lose," says Steve morosely.

I think for a moment and say, "We're losers now. Everyone keeps calling us that. So the worst that can happen is — we won't just be losers. We'll be Miss Little's Losers."

6 THE *NEW* BRUNSWICK VALLEY SCHOOL SOCCER TEAM

I can't believe this. It's Wednesday after school and we're in Miss Little's kindergarten classroom. I feel as though we're all in kindergarten again.

Miss Little sent a message around earlier telling us to meet in her classroom before practice. While we waited for everyone to arrive, she gave us permission to play with the kindergarten stuff as long as we cleaned up after ourselves. No wonder we always find excuses to visit her classroom. It has these tiny chairs and weirdly shaped tables that fit together — they're hexagonal, Shay says — and you bang your knees on them as you walk around if you're not careful. There are three easels in the classroom with trays holding pots of bright red, yellow, and blue paint, as well as big, thick brushes, and the reading corner has a rug to sprawl on. There's hardly any wall without something stuck on it — kids' paintings, poems, letters of the alphabet. The shelves lining one wall are crammed full of games and puzzles and building blocks and Plasticine and scraps of material and coloured pattern blocks and string. The opposite wall has a line of pegs where the kindergarten kids hang their little bookbags. Beside the reading corner rug, Miss Little has a flip chart where she's written the kindergarten news of the day. I read it and discover that Cody has a new cat, Elizabeth has a new baby brother, Katie fell off her bicycle, and Isaac threw up last night.

Shay makes straight for the shape puzzle, where you have to put all these wooden shapes into their corresponding slots on a board. He finishes it off in about half a second, then sits and gazes at Julie, who's playing in the Wendy house. Poor Shay. He couldn't bring himself to ask Julie if she'd keep playing on the team. In the end, he made me come with him to ask her. Then he nearly passed out when he saw her.

"What's the problem?" I asked him.

I knew the answer.

"She's, like, a goddess," he muttered.

I'm not sure what a goddess looks like, but if it's anything like a fairy princess — well, that's what Julie makes me think of. I remember an old fairy tale picture book in Miss Little's classroom. I can't remember what the story was, but I remember this picture of a fairy princess, who was tall, with an oval face, and lots of curly golden hair. And that's what Julie looks like. Mind you, she doesn't act like a fairy princess on the soccer field. She plays midfield and turns into a gorilla. If I was a striker and she was coming to tackle me, I'd just give her the ball.

When I said he could still ask her, even if she was a goddess, Shay said, "But I'm too shy."

I said, "Okay. I'll ask her."

"No, I want to ask her," Shay insisted.

"Well, go and ask her."

"But I'm too shy."

"Okay, I'll ask her."

"No, I want to ask her."

"Well, go and ask her."

"But I'm too shy."

"Okay, I'll ask her."

"No, I want to ask her."

"Well, go and ask her."

"But I'm too shy."

We would have gone on like this forever if I hadn't called, "Yo, Julie. Shay wants to ask you something."

Julie was in a huddle with her friend, Linh-Mai. They giggled. Shay blushed. He didn't say anything. He couldn't. He was paralyzed.

So I said, "He wants to ask you if you'll stay on the soccer team. There's a practice after school today."

Julie said, "Awesome. I'll be there. Thanks for telling me, Shay."

Shay did manage to gasp, "You're welcome."

He's still gazing at her. Jillian and Jessica are painting, their heads bobbing as they talk and giggle, making their identical blond pony tails swing. Silas and Jason are building a fort with the building blocks. I look at the books. Most of them have only one word on the left-hand page and a picture on the right-hand page, but some have real stories. I find my old favourite — *Toby the Terrific Truck That Tried* — and I'm in the middle of it when Miss Little claps her hands and says, "I think we're all here, so it's time to begin. Clean up after yourselves, then come and sit down, children."

She sits on one of the tiny kindergarten chairs in the reading corner and without thinking we all sit on the rug in front of her. I expect her to start with the news of the day, but instead she says, "Let's all welcome our new team member, Brian."

We obediently chant, as if we've been coached, "Welcome, Brian."

We roll our eyes and pretend we're fooling around chanting 'Welcome, Brian' like this, but really we're not. We can't help ourselves, even Silas and Jason and Nicholas, who say it in big, singsong voices. We know Miss Little wants us to say this — so we say it.

Brian's very happy to be here. If he wasn't here, he'd be in detention for Ms. Watkins for not paying attention when we were doing French. I daydream, but look as though I'm paying attention. Brian, on the other hand, fidgets around. This gets him in trouble all the time.

With Brian here, Shay's going to get a surprise in a minute — a nice one, I hope. Brian's going to take Shay's place as goalkeeper. I know about this because I was with Miss Little when she discovered Brian might be good in goal.

This is how it happened: Earlier today, Miss Little and I were in the hallway when Brian walked past. You know how most kids can't walk through a door without jumping up and touching the top of the door frame? It drives some teachers crazy, but we can't help it. It's like a reflex action. Well, Brian wasn't jumping up and touching the tops of doors, because there weren't any along that stretch of hallway. Instead, he was jumping up and touching the *ceiling*. He was like a walking jack-in-the-box. One second he was on the ground, the next he was flying through the air and touching the ceiling. And not just touching it, but, like, staying in the air, as if he was hanging from the ceiling. I'd never seen him do it before. I couldn't believe it. Neither could Miss Little. She said, "Goalkeepers have to jump around, don't they, Toby?"

"That's good, Miss Little. You're learning," I said.

Then she said, "You're friends with Shay, aren't you? Tell me in confidence — does he like playing goal?"

I told her about Shay's granddad being a famous goalkeeper, and Shay feeling he should be a goalkeeper, too, to please his granddad.

"But does Shay *want* to play in goal?" Miss Little asked.

"I don't think so," I told her.

Miss Little looked back at Brian — he was hanging

from the ceiling again — and said, "Hmmm."

After we welcome Brian, Miss Little claps her hands and says, "Now, children, can anyone guess what today is?"

Her glasses have slipped down her nose and she looks at us over the top of them. We know this isn't the sort of question we have to come up with a right answer to. If it was any other teacher asking us what day it is, I would say, "It's the day after yesterday." But this is Miss Little, so I chorus with the others, all of us using singsong voices, "No, Miss Little."

This is too much for Nicholas. He mutters, "We're not in kindergarten now, you know."

Steve quickly reprimands him: "You mustn't be rude."

"Says who?"

"Says the captain — alright?"

Miss Little says, "Thank you, Steve. Now I'll go on. Today is ... " — Miss Little pauses, smiling — "Today is the first practice of the *new* Brunswick Valley School soccer team."

We don't understand.

Steve says, "What's new about it?"

"What's new is — it's going to be a success."

"You mean you think we'll actually win a game? It'd be the first of the season," Silas snorts.

Steve frowns at him, but Miss Little goes on, "I didn't say the team would win. I said the team would be a success."

"Doesn't that mean we win?" asks Jason.

"There's a difference, and that's something we have to talk about," says Miss Little. "The *new* Brunswick Valley School soccer team will not only play according to the rules of soccer, whatever they are, but will also play according to the rules we all learned in kindergarten. If we follow these rules, we will be successful, whether we win or lose. Now, children," Miss Little leans forward, clasping her hands under her chin, "does anyone remember our kindergarten rules?"

This is like a test. Of course, the first thing you do when you have a test is forget everything you ever learned, especially what you learned for the test.

"Shall I start you off?" Miss Little asks.

"I don't think we're going to start ourselves," I say.

"Very well. Our first kindergarten rule is — Be Nice to One Another."

Shay puts his hand up and sputters, "Oh … oh … oh … " as if he's going to throw up or lay an egg. At last he gets out, "I remember another one: Always Do Your Best."

Now I'm remembering, too, and I wave my arm and say, "Oh … oh … oh … "

"Yes, Toby dear?" says Miss Little.

"Share, Share, Share."

"Well done, Toby and Shay."

We look around grinning. It's always nice when Miss Little is pleased with you.

"Can anyone else remember any of our kindergarten

rules? Jessica and Jillian, what did you have to do when you finished painting?"

The twins look at each other, at the painting easel, at Miss Little, then back at each other. They chant together, "Clean Up After Yourself."

Miss Little claps her hands. She's getting really excited now. "I'm so proud of you all remembering our rules. There are just two more. Let's see — Jason and Silas, what did you have to think about when you finished with the building blocks and put them on the wrong shelf?"

Jason and Silas look at the floor as they mumble, "Keep Things in Their Proper Place."

There's one more rule and we can't remember it.

"It's the most important rule," says Miss Little helpfully.

We don't want to disappoint her. I'm wracking my brains and two words suddenly pop into my mind and I gasp, "Dignity and … and … and … Grace."

Miss Little beams. "Well done, Toby. The last rule is — Do Everything with Dignity and Grace. Now I wonder whether you can remember the little rhyme we used to recite to help us remember about dignity and grace."

Like magic it comes back and we chorus, "Grace and dignity, dignity and grace; doesn't matter if you're top, nor who sets the pace. What matters most is not who wins, but how you run the race. So conduct yourself with dignity, dignity and grace."

Miss Little is almost falling off her chair with excitement.

"That's wonderful, children. I'm so proud of how you remember our rhyme. Now —" she claps her hands again, "it's time for our practice, and today we're going to pay special attention to our first three rules — Be Nice to One Another, Always Do Your Best, and Share, Share, Share. Be Nice to One Another means you'll congratulate and encourage one another every chance you get — and you certainly won't criticize. Always Do Your Best speaks for itself. And Share, Share, Share means you won't keep the ball to yourself, like you tell me you used to in the games before the *new* Brunswick Valley team, but you'll give it to one another. Share, Share, Share means pass, pass, pass."

As we leave the classroom, Miss Little quietly asks Shay, "Do you like playing goal?"

"It's okay."

"Are you good at it?"

"Not really. But my granddad likes me to play goal — he used to be a goalkeeper — and no one else would do it."

"Would you like to play a different position?"

Shay says, "Please!"

We go out to the back field. It's not really a soccer field. It's just a field. There aren't any lines on it, but that's no problem because the ball counts as out on one side when it goes into the alders, and on the other when it goes into the ditch. The only way you can tell that the back field is a soccer field is by the goalposts at each end. Mr. Cunningham used to say you could graze sheep on the back field and they'd be very happy. It's not a bad idea. At least they'd keep the grass short. The only thing that keeps it from getting really long is us kids running all over it.

Brian goes in goal and Steve starts to organize us for a five-a-side scrimmage, each side taking turns to attack and defend the goal. Suddenly we realize this team has a problem: we have only ten players, and a soccer team is supposed to have eleven. Julie's friend, Linh-Mai, has come to watch and is standing on the edge of the field. Linh-Mai has twinkly black eyes and long black hair, and is only as tall as Julie's shoulder. When she stands beside Julie, she looks like an elf beside the fairy princess.

"Can Linh-Mai play?" Julie asks.

"Well — *can* Linh-Mai play?" Steve responds sarcastically.

"Steve, dear — rule number one," Miss Little warns him.

"Sorry, Miss Little. Sorry, Julie. Sorry, Linh-Mai," Steve mutters.

Julie waves Linh-Mai onto the field. "What did he say about me?" I hear Linh-Mai whisper to Julie. She's looking at Steve.

Julie lies, "He said he's glad you're playing."

Linh–Mai smiles at Steve. He doesn't notice.

We start the practice. The first thing Linh–Mai does is kick the ball with the front of her foot instead of the side, and the ball flies off at a ninety-degree angle.

"You should see her with a loaf of bread," I wise-crack. "She slices that even better."

I get a warning look from Miss Little. I'm already forgetting kindergarten rule number one.

Miss Little calls, in a singsong voice, "Toby, dear — Being nice to one another is easy to *do*. It makes everyone feel good — and that includes *you*."

I say, "Yes, Miss Little. Sorry, Miss Little," and correct myself: "Good effort, Linh–Mai. You'll get it next time."

Then Steve misses a goal and Silas taunts, "See those white posts with the net behind them, Steve? That's called a goal and you're supposed to put the ball in it, not behind it." All Miss Little has to do is catch his eye and give a little disappointed shake of her head for Silas to say, "I mean — tough luck, Steve. Nice try."

Throughout the practice time we're running around as if there's a swarm of hornets after us. "Doing your best is like breathing, children. It's easy, and it's necessary," Miss Little reminds us from the side of the field. If we lose the ball, we chase after the person who took it off us and try to get it back. When we get the ball, we think, Share, Share, Share, and it's as if the ball is red–hot, and we pass it quickly. In goal, Brian is making some spectacular saves, hurling himself around as if he's got springs in his legs. Only Shay looks a bit out of things. He doesn't know whether he wants to be a forward or a back.

After half an hour Miss Little says, "That's enough for today, children. We mustn't overdo it. Tomorrow is a big day. We have our first game of the playoffs."

As we come off the field she notices Shay's worried look and says, "Would you rather be in goal?"

Shay says, "No. I feel strange with the ball not coming at me all the time, like it does when I'm in goal, but I'll get used to it."

He still looks doubtful so Miss Little prompts him. "And … ?"

"And I'm afraid my granddad will be disappointed that I'm not in goal, like he used to be."

Miss Little says, "We'll fix things. Don't worry."

7 LINES, PATTERNS, SPACE — AND SHAY

After supper Conrad says, "Your turn to wash up, big guy," and goes outside to rake leaves. Ma goes out to watch him.

"Right."

I'm thinking about my geometry homework, which I don't know how to do. This is always happening to me. When I'm in class, I know how to do it, but when I get home, it doesn't make sense. Thinking about geometry reminds me of shapes and space, which brings Shay to mind. Perhaps I'll go down to Shay's and get him to help me with the geometry homework. But I don't want to disturb him and his granddad. This is the sort of thing about having friends that worries me. Does it mean I can just visit when I like? Sometimes it's easier not having friends, so you don't have these things to worry about.

I'm still thinking all this when Ma comes back in and says, "I thought you were washing up, lovey."

"Sorry. I was daydreaming," I say.

Ma says, "You can daydream all you like when the washing up's done."

Have Shay and Ma been talking? First Shay says I can't daydream when I'm playing soccer, and now Ma's bugging me not to daydream at home when there are chores to be done. It was easier when I just had me to worry about — me and my running, and me and my room. Then I could daydream all I liked. Now I have to worry about a whole soccer team, and all sorts of friends, and a whole house.

"By the way," says Ma, "don't forget you're going to tidy the living room like I asked you to do yesterday, and help Conrad rake the leaves, like he asked you to do on Saturday."

See what I mean?

"Yes, Ma."

So I wash up, move a couple of cushions in the living room, and rake three leaves.

Conrad says, "Don't overdo it."

Afterward, I go down to Shay's house. The lights are on in the flower shop, so I guess Shay and his grand-dad are in there. As I open the door, I hear Shay shout, "Check!" and Mr. Sutton says, "You got me again." They're playing chess. When they're not playing chess they're doing jigsaw puzzles. Shay is a whiz at both. I've never seen anyone do jigsaw puzzles like him. He gets this glazed look in his eyes, like when he's surveying the soccer field, except that he's surveying all the puzzle pieces not put in, and all the spaces to be filled, and suddenly he puts in three or four pieces all at once.

Shay and I sit in the corner doing our geometry homework — well, Shay does it and I copy it — while his granddad does his own mathematics homework, working on the flower shop accounts. After a bit he says, "I don't think we'll have any more customers today. How about we close up and make some tea, boys?"

"That'd be nice," I say.

"What's soccer players' favourite tea?" he asks.

We shrug. We know there's a joke coming.

"Penal-tea," says Mr. Sutton.

We laugh politely. Mr. Sutton has to sit down he's laughing so much. Then he asks, "What sort of tea shall we have? Do you like Assam?"

"It's all Assam to me," I quip.

Mr. Sutton staggers around laughing at my little joke. He's still chuckling as he walks to the door to close up. He's just grabbing the "Sorry, We're Closed" sign when the door opens and in walks — Miss Little.

She beams at us. "Shay, Toby, what a lovely surprise. How are you?"

I say, "Yo, Miss Little."

We stand and I nudge Shay, whispering, "It's your home. You have to do introductions."

Shay mumbles, "Hi, Miss Little. This is my granddad. Granddad, this is Miss Little. She used to be our kindergarten teacher and now she's our soccer coach."

Mr. Sutton shakes Miss Little's hand. "If I can do anything to help, you just let me know. I used to be a bit of a soccer player, you know. I used to play in goal."

He points to an old photograph on the wall behind the counter. It's Mr. Sutton's team the year they won some big championship. If you look carefully you can make him out in the middle of the back row, with his arms folded, wearing his green goalkeeper's sweater.

Miss Little nods and smiles, pretending she doesn't know about him being a famous goalkeeper. Mr. Sutton's lost in thought gazing at the picture, so Shay says, "Do you want some flowers, Miss Little? You can help yourself."

Miss Little chooses some flowers and passes them in a bunch to Shay, who's behind the counter now, looking just like his granddad. As he wraps paper around the bouquet, he gets the glazed look in his eyes again and rearranges some of the flowers.

Miss Little gasps. "That's wonderful, Shay. How did you do that?"

Shay looks blank and Miss Little repeats, "How did you know to do that — to move those flowers around like that?"

He shrugs. "I just looked at them and did it. Shall I move them back?"

"No. You've made the bouquet look so much better. You must have an exceptional awareness of space and patterns," says Miss Little, still looking at the flowers.

Shay shrugs again.

I put in, "That's all he sees — shapes and patterns and space. That's why he's a space cadet."

Miss Little takes the flowers and pays, adding, "What position in soccer needs someone who's especially aware of space?"

Mr. Sutton replies instantly, "That'd be your midfielders."

"We need a good midfielder," Miss Little says. "Would you play midfield for us, Shay, instead of in goal?"

I look at Mr. Sutton, wondering how he's going to take this. I needn't worry.

"A good midfielder is vital," he says. "We used to call them halfbacks — right half, left half, and centre half. It's one of the most important positions on the field. A good midfielder can control the game, set up scoring chances — even score sometimes — and marshal the defence. I can see you playing midfield, Shay. You've got the vision for it. You'd be like a young Bobby Moore, the old England centre half. He was one to control the game. He was like a rock. I remember playing against him once. That would be in — let me see — 1968, in London, England. It was raining cats and dogs that day. We were winning one to nothing late in the game when …"

Miss Little winks at Shay, takes her flowers, gives a little wave to me, and quietly leaves.

8 SUPERSTRIKE

We nervously climb off the bus at Keswick Narrows Memorial School for our first playoff game. Miss Little claps her hands. "Gather round, children," she calls.

Steve, glancing at some Keswick Narrows kids nearby, says, "I wish you wouldn't call us children, Miss Little."

Miss Little frowns. "What am I supposed to call you?"

Good question. If we're not children, what are we? I think of how they classify books for us in the library, and say, "How about young adults?"

Miss Little tries it. She claps her hands and says, "Gather round, young adults."

We shake our heads quickly. It doesn't sound right. It makes us sound like a bunch of dorks.

Steve suggests, "Call us children — but say it quietly."

Miss Little says, "I'm sorry — er — children." She whispers 'children.' "I didn't mean to offend you, but I just can't think of you any other way."

Shay sidles up to her and mutters, "We all love you, you know, Miss Little."

She smiles.

The Keswick Narrows Memorial coach, Mr. Patmore, comes over with some of his players. His track suit matches his team's uniforms, and he has his baseball cap on backwards. "Where's your coach?" he asks.

Miss Little pushes her glasses back on her nose. "I am the coach," she says.

Mr. Patmore's eyes widen. I hear one of the Keswick Narrows players say, "This is going to be even easier than we thought."

Mr. Patmore leads his team onto the field for the warm-up. There's quite a crowd from the school watching from the sidelines, this being the first game of the playoffs. Our only supporters are Shay's granddad and Natasha, who's friends with Linh-Mai and Julie. Mr. Patmore lines his team up in two rows. One by one, the players weave through the lines, passing backwards and forwards as they go. It's slick. The home supporters cheer the drill. Then the team stands in a big circle and the players take turns dribbling the ball, going in and out of the other players. Every now and then Mr. Patmore roars, "Shoot!" and whoever has the ball spins around and fires it across the circle. The Keswick Narrows crowd cheers every time someone shoots. We stand on the edge of the field gawking at this. The drill is so perfect it's scary. If it's designed to make us nervous, it's working.

Our coach claps her hands and says quietly, "Gather round, children."

"Are we going to do a show-off drill?" Silas asks.

"No," says Miss Little. "Our only pre-game drill is to remember the things we practised yesterday. Say them with me — quietly, of course."

We chant, "Be Nice to One Another. Always Do Your Best. Share, Share, Share."

"And?" prompts Miss Little.

We look around, hoping no one can hear us, and chorus, "Grace and dignity, dignity and grace; doesn't matter if you're top, nor who sets the pace. What matters most is not who wins, but how you run the race. So conduct yourself with dignity, dignity and grace."

Miss Little nods and smiles, pushing her glasses back on her nose, and says quietly, "Enjoy your game, children."

As we run onto the field, Natasha whoops and applauds. We look over at her and smile gratefully. She does a sort of dance as she cheers, skipping backwards and forwards and waving her arms. She looks impressive. She has black hair — I mean *really* black hair — done in tight crinkles, with little curly bits hanging down each side of her face like Christmas decorations, and she wears a tiny gold ring in her right nostril. Shay's granddad joins in — whooping and applauding, not dancing — but he and Natasha are soon drowned out by the Keswick Narrows supporters, who chant, "Lo-sers. Lo-sers."

The chant grows even louder five minutes into the game when the ball comes to Linh-Mai, who tries to pass to Julie but miskicks the ball. It flies up and hits Linh-Mai in the face. She falls over backwards. I run over to see if she's alright and the Keswick Narrows forward I was supposed to be marking gets the ball and fires it at our goal. Brian flings himself desperately at the ball, but it goes past him into the net.

In the old days, before Miss Little, we would have been insulting each other now. Instead, Silas joins me beside Linh-Mai, saying, "That would have been a good pass," and Jillian runs over and says, "Are you hurt?" Julie hauls Linh-Mai to her feet. She looks a bit dazed but she'll be okay. Miss Little and Mr. Sutton are coming on the field. We wave them away. The referee points to centre.

We're down 1–0 already and the game's hardly started.

The chant starts again: "Lo-sers. Lo-sers."

Miss Little has her hands each side of her face. Mr. Sutton stands beside her and pats her shoulder.

"Go, Brunswick Valley!" Natasha shouts.

The Keswick Narrows students, hearing her, laugh and chant louder, "Lo-sers. Lo-sers."

I feel sorry for Natasha, the only Brunswick Valley School student who's come to watch, bravely shouting her support for us. I'm afraid we're letting her down, a goal behind already. We're letting Shay's granddad down, too, who Shay said could come and watch us again because he thought we were going to play better now.

And of course we're letting Miss Little down. We really are Miss Little's Losers.

In fact we're not just losers. We're double losers. We're losers because we're going to lose the game. And we're losers because we're letting down Miss Little, and Mr. Sutton, and Natasha.

But wait.

Something's happening down at the other end of the field. I have to stop daydreaming and concentrate on the game. Jessica's got the ball and has slipped past the Keswick defence. She's racing towards their goal. Steve and Silas are already lurking there in case she wants to pass. Two Keswick Narrows players are in front of her now. I hear Miss Little's voice in my head — am I imagining it, or is she really shouting it? — "Share, Share, Share." Jessica seems to hear it too, and before the opposing players tackle her she passes to Silas. He stumbles and loses the ball to a Keswick back, but before his opponent can get away, Silas tackles him back. I hear Miss Little's voice again: "Always Do Your Best." Silas has the ball now. He passes to Steve, who lashes the ball at the Keswick Narrows goal.

It flies just over the crossbar.

Mr. Sutton had his hands in the air ready to applaud a goal. Instead he puts them over his head in disappointment. Miss Little is smiling and holding her hands towards us, her arms out straight, giving us two thumbs up.

Natasha does a cartwheel and shouts, "Go, Brunswick Valley!"

The Keswick Narrows chant starts again, drowning out Natasha: "Lo-sers. Lo-sers." But it sounds less certain now.

We settle down for some serious soccer in a way we never have before. We run and hustle, and we encourage one another. Miss Little calls to us, "Share, Share, Share means we care, care, care," so we pass, pass, pass. I even make space for Shay to send the ball back to me when he has his own space closed down. I think he's proud of me. He's playing midfield, and has sent passes where no one has been, not our side or Keswick Narrows. When he does this, the Keswick Narrows supporters laugh and applaud, making fun of him. It doesn't seem to bother Shay. He keeps doing it, and I see Steve looking thoughtfully at him now whenever he has the ball.

In the second half, Keswick Narrows attack us nonstop. I'm really busy on defence and don't have time to even think about daydreaming.

Brian is amazing in goal. He rushes out and blocks a hard shot by the Keswick Narrows centre. When the centre gets the ball he has the whole goal to aim at. By the time he goes to kick the ball, Brian is rushing out at him. This is called "Cutting Down the Angles." We learned it in math class with Mr. Cunningham. Well — Brian learned it. The rest of us, except Shay, didn't really understand. The lesson was supposed to be about acute and obtuse angles, but it turned into a goalkeeping lesson when Mr. Cunningham drew a diagram on the chalkboard. He drew a goal, a striker coming straight at it, and a goalkeeper.

"That's you in goal, Brian," he said.

Brian was drumming on his desk with his hands and doing a sort of sitting-still dance with his feet. He stopped and said, "Wha ... ?"

"That's you, Brian," Mr. Cunningham repeated. "You're on your goal line." He drew lines from the striker to the goalkeeper and to each side of the goal and said, "What sort of angles are they?"

"Big ones," Brian answered.

"Right," said Mr. Cunningham. "Now — suppose Brian the goalkeeper moves closer to the striker. What happens?" He changed the diagram.

"The angles get smaller," Brian said.

"More ... " Mr. Cunningham prompted.

"More — er — acute," Brian supplied.

"Right again," said Mr. Cunningham. "And small angles — acute angles — are much harder to shoot at, of course. It's called 'Cutting Down the Angles.'"

Brian was motionless, studying the diagram. We'd never seen him sit so still for so long. The next class was French, with Ms. Watkins, and in less than five minutes she sent him out into the hallway for bouncing around.

So — after Brian cuts down the angle and stops the ball, it bounces out to another Keswick Narrows forward, who scoops it over Brian's head. I'm sure it's going to be goal number two, but somehow Brian throws himself upwards and backwards at the same time, and manages to tip the ball over the bar.

We're so tired all we can do now is kick the ball upfield when we get it so we can grab a breather before Keswick Narrows attacks again. Here they come now. I rush out to close the space on my side as a Keswick forward approaches. He goes to pass and I stick my leg out. The ball hits my knee and bounces to Shay. He sends it on to Julie. She's been doing her gorilla act on defence and the Keswick players are a bit in awe of her. They back away. They don't know she's exhausted and can hardly move. She manages a pass to Steve. He passes to Silas and races up the field. Silas sweeps the ball out to the wing, where Jessica, on the run, sends it back to Steve. We've caught Keswick Narrows off guard. They've been so busy attacking our goal they've forgotten to defend their own — until now. Their backs are closing in on Steve, but before they get to him he shoots low and hard. The Keswick Narrows goalkeeper dives for the ball. His fingertips touch it, but it's going too fast for him to stop. The ball squeezes past him and into the net.

I can't believe it.

We've scored.

Steve throws his arms into the air. Mr. Sutton roars, "Goooooal!" Natasha does cartwheels and chants, "Go, Brunswick Valley!" Miss Little smiles and claps her hands. The twins giggle and hug. Julie does a forward roll. Shay grins. Linh-Mai smiles at Steve. He doesn't notice.

The referee blows the whistle for the end of the game. It's a 1–1 tie.

As we troop off the field, exhausted but happy, Miss Little greets us. "I'm so proud of you all. You played well, children, and you played with ... "

We finish for her. " ... dignity and grace."

"Dignity and grace," she repeats, clasping her hands in front of her.

"Super strike," Shay's granddad says to Steve.

"That's what we should call him," I say, "Superstrike."

We like the sound of it: Superstrike Steve.

"And in goal — you were flying, Brian," Miss Little says.

The twins giggle and say, "Flyin' Brian."

We like the sound of that, too.

Mr. Patmore shakes hands with Miss Little and says, "Congratulations, er — coach. Beginner's luck, eh?"

Steve snarls, "Good coaching, you mean."

Miss Little reprimands gently, "That's okay, Steve." Then she gives him a little hug. He doesn't pull away. She asks, "Is something bothering you, Steve, dear?"

"Mr. Patmore — he's like my dad," Steve blurts out, "the way he thinks about a woman coaching soccer. I don't dare tell him you're our coach. He'll say you don't know what you're doing. He'll go nuts. I don't think he'll let me play if he finds out."

9 YOU'RE BEING COACHED BY YOUR *KINDERGARTEN TEACHER?*

"Remember: Clean Up After Yourself," says Miss Little.

We're heading onto the back field for the next game of the playoffs and this is the kindergarten rule we have to pay special attention to today.

When Miss Little reminded us about the rule at practice yesterday, we were all puzzled.

"I don't get it," said Linh-Mai.

We thought some more, then Steve blurted out, "I've got it! It means if you mess up — fix it."

"Yeah, like, if you lose the ball, go get it back," Nicholas added.

"Exactly," said Miss Little. "Cleaning Up After Yourself is like eating a hard candy with a hot centre. It's hard getting started, but you get a nice warm glow deep inside you when you finish."

The Pleasant Harbour Consolidated School team is waiting for us on the field. The game's at Brunswick Valley, so we have a few more supporters from our school, curious to see what's happened to us. We've been getting some funny looks since Mr. Walker announced in assembly that we tied Keswick Narrows. It's the first game we haven't lost. The kids can't believe it. The twins' mom is watching, too. She forgot they had a game, so when she arrived after school to pick them up as usual, she stayed to watch.

Natasha has persuaded a couple of friends to join her as cheerleaders for us. Shay's granddad made them pompoms — he's good at that stuff — and they're waving them and chanting, "Brunswick Valley — all the way!" There is a very different feeling in the air from when we were losing all the time. Now it's as if people expect us *not* to lose. I begin to understand how Steve and Shay feel, the pressure of it all. I'm not sure I like it when the game starts, but midway through the first half I begin to feel better. That's when Jessica goes to kick the ball, misses it, and falls over. Instead of giving up and lying on the ground complaining, she giggles, jumps up, runs after the Pleasant Harbour player who took the ball away, and gets it back. She's *cleaning up after herself*. She winds up to kick it again and this time she connects. The ball lands at Shay's feet and he runs towards the Pleasant Harbour goal with it. As he approaches, he veers off to one side, and just when I think he may be pulling a "Toby" — not concentrating and being anywhere on the field except where he should be — I understand what he's doing. He's making space! And guess who's running into the space he's making.

That's right — Superstrike Steve. Too late, the Pleasant Harbour defenders realize what's happening. Shay sends the ball into the space left open by the defenders chasing after him, and with no one to challenge him, Superstrike doesn't break stride as he slams the ball into the net.

Miss Little applauds and beams. Shay's granddad cheers. Natasha and her friends do cartwheels and shout, "Brunswick Valley — all the way!"

We're delirious. We've never been in the lead before. I see us winning the game, and the next, and getting to the provincial finals. I see us becoming famous, and our games being shown on television. I'll sign autographs for the fans before every game. They'll chant, "Toby! Toby!" as I march on the field.

"Toby. Toby!"

Like that.

"Toby! TOBY!"

That sounds like Linh-Mai.

"TOBY! TOBY!"

Uh-oh. Where am I? I've wandered way out of position. The Pleasant Harbour forwards are closing in on our goal and I'm supposed to be there to stop them. I think — Clean Up After Yourself, Toby. I race in to help. One of the Pleasant Harbour forwards shoots. It's a hard, chest-high shot. Flyin' Brian dives and parries it but can't hold it. The ball bounces loose. I get to the ball just before the Pleasant Harbour striker and kick it clear.

Or so I think.

I haven't noticed another Pleasant Harbour player lurking outside the penalty area. She shoots. The ball flies past me. Brian can't see it coming because chubby me is standing in the way and it flies past him into the net.

I'm horrified.

I should have stuck to cross-country running and never tried soccer, so I wouldn't have friends to let down like this. It's easier to be alone, once you get used to it. Friends, like the soccer team, are a worry. I mean — what do you have to *do* with friends, apart from not let them down? I asked Shay that once: If I'm friends with all the soccer team (he said I was), then what do I have to *do*? He said, "Just be yourself."

I said, "But — who is myself?"

Well — right now I know who myself is. Myself is the one who's just messed up badly. I keep apologizing. "Sorry, Brian. Sorry, Miss Little. Sorry, everyone."

"It wasn't your fault," says Brian.

"Never mind," shouts Mr. Sutton.

Miss Little looks as if she wants to run onto the field and hug me, but she just mouths at me. I can make out what she's mouthing. She's saying, "Dignity and Grace, Toby." I nod. I won't get mad and give up, like I would have done before Miss Little was our coach, and neither will the team. I make sure I'm in position for the kickoff, and get through the rest of the game without messing up again. We finish tied at 1–1, and I feel bad that if it wasn't for my mistake we would have won — our first game of the season.

Correction: our first game *ever*.

Again, I find myself apologizing to everyone.

The Pleasant Harbour players applaud us and shake hands at the end of the game. We applaud back. Pleasant Harbour is a little town, about the size of Brunswick Valley, and they understand our struggles. Their coach says, "Good luck in your next game," and shakes hands with Miss Little.

Miss Little stops me. "You made one little mistake — getting out of position — but you corrected it. You Cleaned Up After Yourself. It was just unlucky there was another Pleasant Harbour forward there."

"Sorry, Miss Little," I say.

"There's nothing to apologize for, dear. I'm proud of how you handled your mistake."

Now Miss Little's sounding like Ma and Conrad. They said they were proud of me last night after I had another go at the living room and the leaves without having to be asked. First I moved the cushions around again, and put away some of my stuff, and even dusted the TV table. Then I went out and raked a few more leaves. They must have been lying in wait for me. When I went inside, Ma squished me against her jiggly tummy and said, "Thank you, lovey. I'm proud of you for helping." Conrad didn't actually say he was proud of me — he never says much — but he smiled his crinkly smile and said, "Thanks," so I know he was.

Miss Little's rules must be catching. I'm even obeying them at home now.

We're walking out of the locker room, Steve, Shay, and me, when Steve suddenly stops, grabs my arm and says, "Get this. We're not bottom of our group."

I've been so upset about flubbing up that I haven't thought of it — but he's right. There are four schools in our group — Pleasant Harbour, Westfield Ridge, Keswick Narrows, and us. It's three points for a win, one for a draw, and, of course, none for losing. We know that Westfield Ridge, who everyone thinks is going to win the group and go to the finals, has beaten Keswick Narrows. That means Keswick Narrows has only the one point for drawing with us, and now we've got two points, one for our tie with Keswick Narrows, and one for our tie with Pleasant Harbour today.

We're still trying to get used to the feeling of not being at the bottom when Steve's dad drives into the car park. He was supposed to come and watch the game.

"Is the game over already, son?" he calls, "I was in a meeting. Sorry I missed it."

"That's okay, Dad."

Steve's used to it.

Steve and his dad are opposites. It's as if Steve sets out to be different from him. Mr. Grant always wears a suit. Steve always wears baggy jeans and oversized sweatshirts. Mr. Grant's sandy hair is slicked down neatly — he has it trimmed and styled at Unisex Elite Styles at the mall every Monday morning, Steve told us — while Steve has his mud-coloured hair hanging over his eyes and ears. Mr. Grant has a little moustache that he has trimmed every Monday, too, Steve says. Once, when he was in the car waiting for Steve, we saw him combing it. He always has his Blackberry with him, and the few times he's made it to a game, he's spent most of the time talking into it.

"How did the game go?" he asks.

"We tied one to one," says Steve.

"Did you score?"

Steve's dad always asks if Steve scored.

Steve nods.

"Good man. That's two draws in a row, isn't it? Things are looking up. I'm going to congratulate your new coach on turning this team around." He heads for the school, expecting Steve to follow.

We're horrified, knowing how worried Steve is about his dad finding out that we're being coached by Miss Little.

"The coach had to leave," Steve says quickly.

Miss Little hasn't left. She's standing just inside the school door, making sure we all set off for home safely.

"Your coach left before you?" Steve's dad says, as if this is something good coaches shouldn't do.

Steve's not a good liar, and he's getting more and more worried. His dad is still walking towards the school. Steve lies desperately, without thinking, "She had an appointment."

His dad stops dead in his tracks. "Did you say ... *she*?"

Steve, biting his lip, nods. Shay and I are rooted.

"So you're being coached by a ... woman?"

Steve nods again.

I wonder why this is such a big deal.

Shay and I are getting uncomfortable. We wish we could creep away, but we want to help Steve.

"Miss Little's a good coach," I say, trying to help.

Uh-oh. I should have kept my mouth shut.

Steve's dad turns on me. "Do you mean you're being coached by ... your *kindergarten teacher*?"

All we can do is nod.

"What does she know about soccer?"

We shrug.

"Does she play soccer?"

We shake our heads.

"Has she *ever* played soccer?"

"Don't think so," says Steve, miserably.

"This is outrageous. Miss Little may know about teaching kindergarten, but she knows nothing about soccer. Now let me make sure I have this clear. The development of my son's soccer talent is in the hands of a kindergarten teacher who knows nothing about the sport. Am I right?"

Steve starts, "Miss Little ... " but his dad interrupts him.

"We'll talk about this at home. Then I'd better talk to Mr. Walker about it. If the school can't provide a proper coach, I think it's best there's no soccer in the school at all, and it's certainly best that you don't play soccer here. I'll arrange for you to play in one of the city leagues."

"But dad..." Steve starts.

"In the car!" Steve's dad barks.

Shay and I look worriedly at one another as they drive away.

"What can he do?" Shay asks.

"He's got influence, being an important business-man and stuff like that," I say. "He gives money to the school, and he's on the parent council. He can tell Mr. Walker he doesn't want the team playing if Miss Little is coaching..."

"Mr. Walker won't give in to him."

"He'll have to if the parent council tells him to. And not just that. He can keep Steve from playing, which means we'll lose our top goal scorer."

"Correction," says Shay. "We'll lose our *only* goal scorer."

10 THRILLED… AND SCARED

A week later, we don't know whether to be thrilled or scared. Both, I think — thrilled one minute, scared the next.

We're thrilled because *we beat Westfield Ridge 3–0.* Now we're in the elimination stage of the provincials, where the winner gets to represent southern New Brunswick in the regional finals.

We're scared as well as thrilled because our opponents in the next round will be — you guessed it — St. Croix Middle School. Not only have we never beaten St. Croix, but they also tease and bully us on the field, and their supporters taunt us from the sidelines. We remember last time we played them. We remember every chant of "Lo-sers. Lo-sers," and the elbows and kicks and trips.

Linh-Mai's not thinking of the next game. She's never played against St. Croix, after all. She's still fixated on our surprise win against Westfield Ridge. She's also still fixated on Steve.

"Your first goal — that was a stunner," she says to him.

Steve doesn't seem to hear. He's been in a sulky mood since his dad discovered that Miss Little is our coach. He's so afraid his dad will pull him off the team that he didn't even tell him about the Westfield Ridge game.

We're in the cafeteria and it's lunchtime and crowded and noisy. The daily special is spaghetti with meat sauce, which is always popular, and although the cafeteria ladies are serving it up as fast as they can, there's still a long lineup. I was late getting to lunch because Ms. Watkins kept me after French class for daydreaming. She said I couldn't spend my life daydreaming. I said I couldn't daydream in soccer because I had let the team down, and I couldn't daydream at home because it stopped me from doing the chores, so school was the only place I had left to do it. Ms. Watkins shook her head and said, "Oh Toby." I said, "Yo, Ms. Watkins," and she let me go. I got the last place at the long table where the rest of the team was. After we've eaten, there is time to talk about our recent victory over Westfield Ridge.

We knew before the game started that Westfield Ridge had only managed a tie with Pleasant Harbour the day before, which meant that if we beat them, we'd win our round-robin group and go through to the elimination round. On the other hand, if they beat us, they'd go through, which is what everybody expected to happen, including us.

The kindergarten rule we practised before the game was Keep Things in Their Proper Place. We didn't understand what that had to do with soccer until Miss Little repeated, looking right at me, "Keep Things in Their Proper Place."

"Oh. Are we the things?" I asked.

Miss Little nodded and said, still looking at me, "Keep Things in Their Proper Place means keep your positions. It means no daydreaming and no wandering around."

"Yes, ma'am," I said.

She ruffled my hair and recited, "Everyone struggles and it's a *disgrace* — when things are not kept in their proper *place*."

"Jeez, Miss Little, where do you find this stuff?" I asked.

The game was held at Westfield Ridge. It's a town between Brunswick Valley and the city of Saint John, and most of the people who live there go into Saint John for work. It's all malls, subdivisions, and golf clubs that don't allow you in unless you wear the right clothes and shoes. We've played Westfield Ridge before, so we know them a bit. They're a decent team — mannerly and fair — and they're very good. Earlier in the season they beat us 10–0. Their goalkeeper only touched the ball twice during the whole game, and that was when her defenders passed back to her.

But this time we were better prepared. By keeping our positions on defence, we stopped every attack. Linh-Mai and I stayed close to our goal so that if Westfield Ridge got past our midfielders they would have to face us. And behind us was Flyin' Brian, leaping around the goal like a jack-in-the-box. Shay and Steve also suddenly seemed to be on the same wavelength, although it was a different wavelength from the rest of us. It was as if they were reading each other's mind. Shay would get the ball — usually from Julie, who was good at stealing it from opposing players — and he'd sort of roll it around under his foot while he surveyed the field. Then he'd kick it into an empty space, or — amazingly — into a space that wasn't empty when he kicked it, but became empty when Westfield Ridge's players reacted to his kick. No one noticed these spaces. No one, that is, except Steve, who somehow knew where Shay was going to send the ball and would be on his way to that empty space.

That's how the first goal came about. Steve got the ball from Shay and passed to Jessica, who quickly passed back for him to blast the ball past the Westfield Ridge goalkeeper. We never looked back after that. Steve scored the other two goals as well. The first came on a penalty shot when a Westfield Ridge defender accidentally tripped Steve in the penalty area, and the last one was brilliant. Steve got the ball from Shay

— they were mind-reading one another again — weaved around two Westfield Ridge defenders, then dribbled the ball past the goalkeeper. This happened late in the game, sealing our win. Steve stood in the goalmouth with his arms in the air. Julie did one of her forward rolls. Shay's granddad and Conrad went wild, dancing around on the touchline and shouting, "Goal, Goal, Goal!" The twins' mom and Julie's mom, who'd helped to drive us over, looked at them as if they were crazy — then joined in. Natasha and the cheerleaders chanted, "Brunswick Valley — all the way!" and did their new routine, starting with leg kicking going into the splits, and ending with cartwheels. Miss Little smiled and clapped her hands.

"It was a stunner," Linh-Mai says again, looking at Steve.

He still doesn't seem to notice.

Mr. Cunningham is on duty in the cafeteria. He comes over to our table and congratulates us in his gruff voice.

Julie is surprised. "Were you watching us?" she asks.

Mr. Cunningham, a bit embarrassed, confesses, "I was watching from my car." He adds, "The St. Croix coach was at the game, too, sizing up his next opponents."

We don't know whether to be flattered or even more scared by this news.

"You were playing with a good sense of position,"

Mr. Cunningham says, leaning forward. "Julie and Shay have a natural partnership."

They both blush. What's going on here? I know Shay would like a "partnership" with Julie, but … do you suppose she'd like a partnership with him too?

Mr. Cunningham says, "Use that partnership. Julie is good at getting the ball" (that's when she does her gorilla act) "and sending it to Shay. As soon as you see Julie with the ball, you midfielders and backs should move up the field, ready to take a pass from Shay. Try and read his intentions as well as Steve does. Now, when Brian has the ball, defenders, you need to move out to the wings to give him the option of passing wide to you … "

"Using the obtuse angles you've created with the goal," Brian puts in.

"Right," says Mr. Cunningham. "Or, if it's important to get the ball upfield fast, Brian will send the ball straight up the centre, because … "

"Because a straight line is the shortest distance between two points," Brian supplies.

"Right," says Mr. Cunningham again.

We gape.

Brian and Mr. Cunningham are having a conversation about mathematics. That's strange enough, because usually in mathematics class Mr. Cunningham and Brian don't have conversations about mathematics; they have conversations about Mr. Cunningham wondering whether Brian could keep still for just one nanosecond. But also — the conversation is taking place not in the classroom, but in the cafeteria, where usually the last thing Brian, or any of us, wants to talk about is mathematics.

Mr. Cunningham is still talking. "The important thing for you all is to make the space on the field work for you."

He looks up guiltily. We haven't noticed Miss Little come in.

Our old coach says to our new coach, a bit embarrassed, "I was just congratulating your team on their win yesterday. I should congratulate you, too, on your coaching."

"You taught them to play soccer. All I'm doing is trying to teach them how to conduct themselves on the field," says Miss Little.

"Whatever you're doing — it's working," Mr. Cunningham replies. "If I can help in any way, let me know. They were driving me crazy," he looks around at us and we smile back innocently, "but I'd still like to help if I can."

Miss Little pulls an extra chair over so she can sit at the head of our table and says, "I came to tell you we won't have a practice this week, children. I want you to save your energy for the game against St. Croix. There's only one more rule I want you to pay special attention to, anyway, and you're doing that already."

We know the last rule. Miss Little always said it was the most important: Do Everything with Dignity and Grace.

"Let's forget about that dignity and grace stuff against St. Croix," says Steve. "They're going to be out to murder us."

We all nod and start telling Miss Little about the last time we played St. Croix. She holds up her hand and we stop talking. It's like magic.

"That makes it all the more important to remember the dignity and grace rule," she says firmly.

We chorus, "Yes, Miss Little."

"Let's say the rhyme now, very quietly. That'll be instead of this week's practice," she says.

We lean forward and chorus, "Grace and dignity, dignity and grace; doesn't matter if you're top, nor who sets the pace. What matters most is not who wins, but how you run the race. So conduct yourself with dignity, dignity and grace."

As we finish, we realize the cafeteria has gone silent. We look up. It must be Creeping Up On People Day. First Miss Little arrives without our noticing, and now Mr. Walker and Steve's dad are standing there.

Steve's mouth drops open and he stutters, "H-hello, Dad." He stands up, then sits back down.

Mr. Grant looks at Mr. Walker, then at Miss Little, then back at Mr. Walker.

Mr. Walker says, "This is our soccer coach, Miss

Little, and some of her team."

Steve's dad glares at Miss Little. "What are you running here — a soccer team or a playgroup?" he booms.

Miss Little stares blankly at Mr. Walker.

Mr. Walker starts, "Mr. Grant..."

Mr. Grant interrupts him. We've learned you never interrupt Mr. Walker, but Mr. Grant does it.

He storms at Miss Little, "I came here to discuss with Mr. Walker some concerns I have about the coaching of the soccer team. I heard some nonsense about the team playing soccer according to rules they learned in kindergarten. I made it clear to Mr. Walker that I wanted my son's soccer talent developed under the direction of a qualified and experienced coach. Mr. Walker assured me you had coaching ability and suggested that I come and talk to you, and I find you here teaching my son kindergarten rhymes instead of soccer tactics."

Mr. Walker repeats, "Now, Mr. Grant..."

But Steve's dad is on a rant and won't be stopped. He points a shaking finger at Steve as he rails at Miss Little: "That's the last time he'll be playing under your coaching, and it's the last time he'll be playing for Brunswick Valley!"

Mr. Grant storms out. Mr. Walker follows him. Steve goes too. Julie puts her arm round Miss Little's shoulders.

The cafeteria is silent. All the kids have stopped eating and are staring at us.

Shay whispers, "Even if Miss Little was a qualified coach, it wouldn't make any difference to Steve's dad. He just doesn't think women should coach soccer."

"He's stuck in the Dark Ages," Linh-Mai says.

We sit in silence. Finally Brian says, "No Steve means no goals means..."

I finish for him, "St. Croix are going to murder us."

We all look at one another. No one speaks, but we're all thinking the same thing.

We really will be Miss Little's Losers this time.

11 DIGNITY AND GRACE

Shay sits at the counter of Sutton's Flowers with his arms spread out and his head resting on them. Julie is pacing around the shop, a fairy princess among the flowers. I'm sitting on an upturned bucket, with my elbows on my knees and my chin resting in my hands — a garden gnome among the flowers.

It's Friday evening, the day before the elimination game against St. Croix Middle School.

Shay's granddad looks at each of us in turn and says, "Come *on*, boys. What's the worst that could happen?" He answers himself. "You could lose — right?"

"We could be embarrassed," says Julie.

"Laughed at," says Shay.

"Humiliated," I add, for good measure.

"You don't even know for sure that Steve's dad won't let him play," says Conrad, who has come down to the shop to help Shay's granddad try and cheer us up. Good luck.

"Steve says his dad won't let him be coached by

a woman who doesn't understand the game and who treats her players like preschoolers," I say for the third time this evening. "He took Steve into the office with him to see Mr. Walker about it, and Steve told us afterwards."

"So we have to play St. Croix without Steve," says Julie.

"*And* with only ten players," says Shay. "The play-off rules say we can't add a new player once they've started."

We've said all this already. It's as if we think if we keep saying it, it will go away.

* * *

Shay's granddad drives us to the game in the flower shop van. Conrad sits in the front with him. Shay, Julie, and me are in the back. It's raining lightly as we set off, and Mr. Sutton and Conrad are still trying to cheer us up.

"Did you hear about the soccer player who always takes a piece of rope on the field with him?" Mr. Sutton asks.

"Why does he take a piece of rope on the field with him?" says Conrad, playing the straight man.

"Because he's the skipper," says Mr. Sutton.

They roar with laughter. We manage a little smile, but we don't say a word during the half-hour drive. We're too nervous.

You drive into St. Croix through a sort of long strip mall of car dealerships, takeouts, building-supply depots, and second-hand stores. After that you're on St. Croix Main Street, and when you get there you wonder why you bothered, because all you see are empty stores with boarded up windows. Just beyond Main Street the subdivisions start, and in the middle of them is St. Croix Middle School, which, like the town, is four times the size of Brunswick Valley. It's funny to think that back when Conrad and Ma were kids growing up in Brunswick Valley, it was the "big" town, and St. Croix was just a little community on the St. Croix River. Then they built the pulp mill and the town grew and grew. Conrad says St. Croix is like a teenager who's grown big and strong but doesn't yet know what he wants to be. Brunswick Valley may not have much — not enough to call itself a town, really, although it does — but with the river running through the middle, and the few little stores clustered there, at least it seems to have a heart.

The traffic is backed up along St. Croix's Main Street because it's shift change at the mill, and as we inch along we grow aware of groups of people walking in the same direction as us. When we turn up the side street that leads through the subdivisions to the school, there are even more people, and we realize they're all going to watch the game. We're the main attraction this Saturday afternoon in St. Croix. This makes us even more scared than we are already. Shay's granddad finds a parking spot at the front of the low, sprawling school.

"We'll be cheering for you," he says, putting one arm round Shay and patting Julie on the shoulder.

Conrad squeezes my shoulder and says, "Go get 'em, big guy."

They join the crowd heading down the path beside the school to the playing field at the back. We see Miss Little and some of the others waiting by the main door. We get some amused looks when she waves to us and calls, "Over here, children."

"Please, Miss L., not so loud," I plead as we join them.

She pushes her glasses back on her nose and whispers, "Sorry, dear."

If she's as nervous as us, she's not showing it. She's as smiley as she always is.

When we're all there, Miss Little says, "Everyone find a partner. Form a line in twos, and follow me."

She leads us into the school. The main hallway goes straight through it to the field behind. We march along behind our coach, our cleats rattling on the tiled floor and echoing off the bare walls. At the end of the long hallway, Miss Little stops. We stop too, peering ahead. Miss Little opens the doors for us.

We gape.

We see all the subdivisions surrounding the field. We see the pitch, where the St. Croix team is already warming up.

And we see spectators, more than we've ever had watching us before. They're lining the field two or three deep. The bleachers on the opposite side are full of St. Croix students.

As soon as they see us, it starts. "Lo-sers. Lo-sers."

We head down the steps to the edge of the field and find the visiting team's area. Shay's granddad, Conrad, and some other parents are beside our bench, with Natasha and the cheerleaders. Natasha's group is chanting, "Brunswick Valley — all the way!" but even from right beside them we can hardly hear them over the roar of, "Lo-sers. Lo-sers."

Miss Little says, "Gather round, children." She says it quietly, but she doesn't have to. No one else is going to hear above the chanting St. Croix kids, who are getting even louder: "Lo-sers. Lo-sers."

"Now, dears," Miss Little says, "I know you're nervous and worried, and I know the game's going to be difficult without Steve, and with only ten of you on the team. But I still want you to remember all the rules we've been practising, because they've served you well, haven't they?"

We nod and chant, "Yes, Miss Little."

She goes on, "And today, no matter what happens in the game, I especially want you to remember the rule, Do Everything with Dignity and Grace. Now — off you go, dears. Enjoy your game."

We're thinking — right, Miss Little, like enjoy our

execution, or enjoy being boiled alive, or enjoy eating this meal of broken glass. But we don't say this. We chorus again, "Yes, Miss Little."

I can feel my wet shirt sticking to my back and shoulders from the drizzle. The muddy field sucks at my cleats as we head out onto it.

Natasha and the cheerleaders do their leg splits and kicking and cartwheels routine, chorusing, "Brunswick Valley — all the way!" and there's some polite applause from the adults around the field, but mostly all we hear is the roar from the bleachers, which gets even louder as the kids stamp and clap with the rhythm of their chant: "Lo-sers. Lo-sers."

I think — we haven't been Miss Little's Losers since I made up the name. But this time, I'm afraid we're going to earn our title.

We're taking our positions — Keep Everything in Its Proper Place — for the starting kickoff. The St. Croix players have their names on their shirts. The three forwards at the centre are Jones, Dougan, and Holt. They're enormous.

As the referee checks her watch, Jones sidles up to Julie and says, "What are you doing after the game, Blondie?"

Julie says — well, I won't tell you what she says — and the St. Croix player comes back with, "You'll be sorry you said that."

Shay's about to move in but Julie mouths, "It's okay."

Shay glares at the St. Croix player. This is not a good start to the game.

The referee checks her watch and blows the whistle to start.

We're in trouble right away. The ball comes to Julie. She's still upset by the exchange with Jones, and she's not concentrating. She keeps the ball too long and the St. Croix players close in on her, leaving her no room to pass. She tries to get the ball back to Brian, in goal, but her pass is too weak, and instead of going to Brian, it trickles to the feet of Jones, who's in the penalty area. Brian moves out to cover him and Jones sends the ball to Dougan, who taps it into the empty net.

"Thanks, Blondie," Jones calls, and runs across to the bleachers with his arms out as if he's just scored in the World Cup. He points to Julie and applauds her.

The kids catch on and start chanting, "Blondie! Blondie!"

We mess up again straight from the restart. Nicholas takes the centre and rolls the ball back to Julie. As she runs to collect it, Jones calls, "Hey, Blondie!" She gets distracted again and misses the ball. It rolls past her to Dougan, who passes to Holt, who shoots and scores.

Only ten minutes have gone and we're already down 2–0. I do a quick calculation: if we keep on like this, and St. Croix score a goal every five minutes, and there are forty-five minutes in each half, that means they'll score nine by halftime, and another nine by the end of the game. Surely we're not going to lose 18–0. That'd be bad even by our old standards.

But we settle down. A sort of grim and desperate resolve gets hold of us. You can almost feel it. We don't do much attacking, and our forwards drop back to help us on defence. We're like a wall stopping the St. Croix forwards. They run at us over and over again, but somehow we hold our positions and stop them. We obey all Miss Little's rules without thinking. We always knew exactly what she wanted us to do when we were in kindergarten. Now, seven years later, we're still doing exactly what she wants us to do. Julie has turned from a distracted fairy princess into a gorilla, and the St. Croix forwards are getting scared of her. They pass as soon as she moves to tackle them. When Shay gets the ball, he doesn't move much, but he keeps it. It's as if it's glued to his foot. He spins around with it, avoiding tackles, until he sees one of us making space for a pass. The St. Croix team is getting frustrated. So are the kids on the bleachers. They thought we were going to be pushovers. When they're not chanting, "Lo-sers. Lo-sers," they're taunting Julie with, "Blondie. Blondie." But she's concentrating so hard she no longer seems to hear them.

She's got the ball now and kicks it clear of our goal. We pause to catch our breath.

"Here they come again," Linh-Mai warns.

Linh-Mai and I stand on either side of the goal,

with Flyin' Brian between us. We're like his bodyguards. He's covered in mud from flinging himself around the goal making one amazing save after another. He's been kicked twice by Jones as he dived for the ball with the St. Croix forwards closing in on it.

The ball is coming high towards us. Julie and Dougan jump to head it. Suddenly Julie's head jerks back and she's lying on the ground. I saw what happened, but the referee didn't. As he jumped, Dougan grabbed her long hair and pulled her backwards, so she fell over as he headed the ball. It goes to Holt, who sets off towards our goal. I move out to close down his space, reminding myself not to commit to a tackle unless I am sure I can get the ball. I force Holt to move wide of the goal. He wants to pass across to Jones but I'm in his way. I hear Brian call, "Stay with him, Toby." My eyes are fixed on the ball. Holt says, "If you want it, blubber boy — here you are," and kicks it as hard as he can straight at me. The ball hits me in the stomach, and air rushes out of me as if I'm a burst balloon. It's replaced by a fierce pain that clutches at my throat and roars around my stomach. I collapse, winded. The referee puts the whistle to her lips as if she's going to blow it to stop the game, but brings her hand down and lets the play continue. I guess getting the ball kicked in your chubby tummy counts as an accident and not a foul. Now Dougan is getting the ball from where it bounced off me. Still on the ground, I swing my leg to try and knock it away from him. He kicks me instead of the ball. Jones rushes in and takes it. Linh-Mai moves over to challenge him, leaving Holt unmarked. Jones passes to Holt, who fires the ball past Brian's desperate and despairing dive.

It's 3–0.

The referee blows her whistle for halftime.

I struggle to a sitting position, still trying to catch my breath. Brian stays down in the mud where he landed. Linh-Mai sinks to her knees, exhausted. She's crying, thinking the last goal was her fault. I gasp, "Hey, Linh-Mai … " It's all I have breath for. Julie is slowly sitting up, holding her neck. Shay plods across to her. He leans with one hand resting on his knee while he pats her shoulder comfortingly with the other. I hear Miss Little's voice. She's moving among us, like an army general among wounded soldiers. She hugs Shay. She kneels before Julie and wipes mud from her face and hair. She bends over Brian and strokes his curly head. She puts her hands on each side of Linh-Mai's face, wipes her tears, and says, "It wasn't your fault, dear. There's no need to cry." She ruffles my hair and says, "Are you alright?"

I nod.

"Shall I help you up?"

I look up at her. "Do you have a crane handy?"

She offers me her hand — it's small and white and has long fingers — and I struggle to my feet. Still holding my hand — I should be embarrassed but for some reason I'm not — she says, "Gather round, children."

When we're standing in a bedraggled, muddy, bruised group around her, she says, "I'm so proud of you."

She leads us off the field. We follow, in a row, like ducklings.

Then something amazing happens.

The crowd starts to applaud. Not the St. Croix kids on the bleachers, who are laughing at us and chanting, "Lo-sers. Lo-sers," but all the rest — they clap for us as we stagger off the field.

"What are they clapping for?" Linh-Mai wonders aloud.

"Don't you know?" says Miss Little.

I know, before she says anything, and I think some of the others know, too.

"They're applauding your dignity and grace."

12 THE MAGIC COMBINATION

Halftime is a ten-minute break. The St. Croix players are clustered around their coach. He has a little white-board and he's drawing on it while they watch. He's demonstrating moves and tactics to use against us in the second half, I guess.

Our coach tells us, "Rest, children."

We sprawl on the ground. Ma arrives and helps Conrad and Mr. Sutton pass around oranges cut in quarters, ready for us to eat.

"I thought you were working," I say to Ma.

"I took time off. I didn't want to miss your big game," she says, patting my cheek. I think I might cry. "How are you doing, anyway?" Ma asks.

"We're down 3–0 and I got the ball kicked in my stomach," I stammer.

"That's nice, lovey," says Ma, moving on with the oranges.

Miss Little is sitting on the ground close to Julie. I hear Miss Little whisper, "You know how good you are at forward rolls ... " Miss Little beckons Jillian over. I think they're plotting something.

Miss Little strolls over to me. "Are you sure you're alright to continue?" she asks.

As she speaks, Mr. Walker arrives with Steve and his dad. Steve is in his soccer gear, ready to play.

Mr. Grant is saying, "This had better convince me."

"It will," Mr. Walker tells him.

Mr. Walker says quietly to Miss Little, but I can't help overhearing, "I persuaded Mr. Grant to watch the team in action, to prove you know what you're doing. If he's not convinced, he's going to complain to the parent council about me, claiming that I'm insulting the players by having them coached by ... by ... "

"By a woman?" says Miss Little.

"By an incompetent girl is what he actually said."

Miss Little raises her eyebrows and says, "Hmmm."

Then she turns back to us, puts her hands just under her chin, and claps for our attention. "Now, children, we're going to do some kindergarten mathematics."

"Miss L.," I murmur, "You're losing it."

"Pay attention, Toby, and everyone," she says. "Before we start the second half, let's talk about the Magic Ten Combinations. Do you remember them?"

Steve's dad scoffs and interrupts. "I'm not having my son spoken to in a soccer game as if he's in a kindergarten class —"

"Enough," snaps Mr. Walker. "I said you could watch

as long as you didn't interfere with the game."

Mr. Grant turns on him: "I hope you realize that my colleagues on the parent council are going to hear about how you're encouraging this nonsense ... "

Steve is hanging his head in embarrassment. We're all embarrassed. Mr. Walker ushers Mr. Grant away.

Miss Little regains our attention: "Children, the Magic Ten Combinations, the special pairs of numbers which add up to ten — do you remember them?"

We look at one other, wondering, then nod uncertainly.

"Well, I want the Magic Ten Combinations not in twos, but in threes."

"You mean — like four and four and two?" I offer.

"Go on."

Silas shrugs. "Seven and two and one."

"I get it," says Julie. "We're talking positions in soccer, aren't we? The Magic Ten Combinations in threes are for three lines of players, and then the goalkeeper is number eleven. So — how about 4-2-4? That means we'd have four forwards, two midfielders, and four defenders."

"Keep going."

Shay glances at his granddad standing nearby, then announces "5-3-2. Five forwards, three midfielders, two defenders." He repeats, thoughtfully, "*Five* forwards."

Miss Little nods. "Let's try playing in a 5-3-2 formation. We have to attack, and we have nothing to lose."

She beckons Mr. Sutton over and says, "Playing 5-3-2 means playing in an attacking sort of way, doesn't it?"

Shay's granddad gleams with excitement. "We played 5-3-2 all the time when I played for Newcastle Wanderers in the old English First Division. We had Bernie Hunter and my old friend Tommy Green on the wings in those days. They were flyers. They'd bring the ball down the wings like lightning, and in the centre waiting for their passes would be the three inside forwards. That was the way to score goals. Why — I remember once we were playing Manchester Albion. That would have been in — let's see — 1966. No — 1967. Yes, 1967 — and we were two goals down, with only fifteen minutes left to play, and ... "

Miss Little gently interrupts him, "Please, we have to get back on the field. Can you help us get organized in a 5-3-2 formation?"

"Oh. uh, right ... " says Mr. Sutton. "Well, Toby and Linh-Mai, you're the two fullbacks. You stay back and protect Brian in goal, like you've been doing."

We nod proudly.

"Julie and Silas, keep playing midfield with Shay. Your job is to control the midfield space. Close it down when St. Croix have the ball. Open it up by making space for yourselves when we're in possession."

"How?" asks Julie.

Mr. Sutton explains. "As soon as we get possession, you and Silas move up and support the five forwards.

You'll be like extra strikers. Shay will hang back so he can be an extra defender if necessary. He'll also keep the ball while you and the forwards make space for yourselves. So use your height — especially you, Julie — to get the ball to Shay. Shay — you know what to do. You do too, Steve, up front. You can roam where you like but keep your eye on Shay. You know what I mean."

We're hanging on Mr. Sutton's every word. We look like a real soccer team getting advice from our coaches.

"Now, twins — you have three strengths," says Mr. Sutton.

"We do?" they say, and giggle.

Mr. Sutton goes on, "Use your three strengths. First, you have your outstanding speed. Use it to fly down the wings with the ball and then get it into the centre, where the inside forwards — you, Steve, and Jason and Nicholas — will be waiting. Second, twins — you kick with different feet. Jillian, you kick with your right foot, and Jessica, you kick with your left foot."

They stare at each other in surprise. The foot they use for kicking is the only difference between them — and it's taken a real soccer player like Mr. Sutton to spot it.

"Your third strength is — you look the same," he says. He grins, and goes on, "so switch sides whenever you like, so the backs marking you don't know which one of you is coming at them and which foot you'll pass or shoot with. You'll be the Interchangeable Twins."

The twins giggle delightedly.

"Jason and Nicholas, play just behind Steve, going for goal when you can. That's all. Over to you, Madam Coach."

We all look from Shay's granddad to Miss Little. Her long blond hair is hanging in soaked rats' tails and her big, round glasses are covered in raindrops.

"And remember, children … " she prompts us.

"The kindergarten rules," we supply.

"And?"

We chant, "Grace and dignity, dignity and grace; doesn't matter if you're top, nor who sets the pace. What matters most is not who wins, but how you run the race. So conduct yourself with dignity, dignity and grace."

As we head out for the second half, we see Steve's dad shaking his head and speaking angrily to Mr. Walker.

But on the field, our new formation begins to take effect. The twins are having fun switching sides every few minutes. I hear them giggling as they exchange positions. The ploy works. The St. Croix defender marking Jessica is totally confused. He thinks Jillian is Jessica and watches her left foot, thinking this is the one she'll pass with. But Jillian kicks with her right foot. Giggling, she sidesteps the tackle intended to neutralize her left foot, and passes with her right. Meanwhile the defender marking Jillian realizes he's marking the wrong winger when Jessica sidles up to him, winks, and says, "You're marking the wrong one." He looks around desperately for Jillian, leaving Jessica unmarked and ready to receive Jillian's pass. She runs towards goal. She wants to pass into the centre but everyone is marked.

"Shoot!" shouts Mr. Sutton.

Jessica tries a long shot. The St. Croix goalkeeper has been looking from Jessica to Jillian, wondering which winger he's facing, and which foot she'll shoot with. While he's still wondering, the ball flies past him.

We've got a goal back. It's 3–1.

"Let's hear it for the twins!" Shay's granddad roars from the touchline. Beside him, Conrad and Ma high-five each other. "Yes!" Mr. Walker shouts, and gives a thumbs-up to Miss Little, who beams.

A few minutes later we're on the attack again, and the ball bounces out of play for a throw-in near the St. Croix goal. The defenders crowd between their goal and the touchline where Julie will take the throw-in. Julie looks across at Miss Little, who nods back. "Excuse me," Julie says to the spectators on the touchline around her, and clears a way through them, stopping way back from the touchline. The surprised spectators fall back, giving her room as she paces out her approach to the line. The kids on the bleachers are laughing at Julie's preparations and are taunting: "Blondie. Blondie." More St. Croix players, curious, come over to fill the space between the line and their goal. Jillian is on the far edge of the crowd of players, watching Julie carefully.

Julie takes a practice run to the line, counting her steps. The referee waves at Julie to stop delaying and take the throw. Julie paces back and trots forward, gathering speed. She does a forward roll, hugging the ball close to herself. As she regains her feet and uncoils, the last parts of the fairy princess to unroll are her arms and her hands, still grasping the ball. She lets it go with her arms at their highest and fastest point, and the combined momentum of her run and her forward roll and her uncoiling enable her to launch the ball over the heads of all the players — all except Jillian, who's been waiting for this. All alone, she gathers the ball and takes it easily past the astonished St. Croix goalkeeper.

3–2.

We're cooking now. We're playing as we've never played before.

But as we play better, St. Croix play even more unscrupulously. Three times Steve gets the ball and is about to shoot when he's tripped. His dad, who's gone from standing on the touchline with his hands in his pockets looking grumpy to cheering us on excitedly, is getting angry at the treatment Steve's getting.

With only five minutes left in the game, we still can't break through. The St. Croix coach calls a time out. He runs onto the field and starts pointing at defensive positions. He's getting his team ready to hold us at bay — at all costs.

"Gather round, children," Miss Little calls to us from the sideline.

She reminds us to continue to play with dignity and grace, no matter how much provocation we receive. "Please, children, do not retaliate. If you play unfairly, you'll regret it. I want you to leave the field as proudly as you went out onto it."

Steve's dad, who winces every time Miss Little calls us children, starts to protest, but Mr. Walker restrains him.

The time out gives St. Croix new momentum and determination. They're not just defending now. They're attacking. They surge forward. Linh-Mai and Brian and I get ready for a last-ditch stand. If they score again we know we have no hope of drawing even. Jones and Dougan come barrelling though our midfielders. Jones lets fly with a hard, high shot. Flyin' Brian leaps and gets one hand behind the ball. He can't hold it and it bounces down to Linh-Mai. Jones, following up his shot, roars towards her. He's like a tank attacking a baby. Linh-Mai desperately punts the ball away, not even looking where she kicks. Luckily, the ball lands at Shay's feet. He sends it smartly on to Steve, who weaves around two St. Croix defenders, then hesitates. I know what Steve's thinking. He's remembering the kindergarten rule about Share, Share, Share, but he's moved so fast our other forwards haven't caught up with him. Miss Little understands, too, and shouts, "It's okay, Steve. You don't have to pass. Go it alone."

Steve gallops toward the goal like a runaway horse.

The defenders are hard on his heels, but he outpaces them and fires the ball past the helpless St. Croix goalkeeper.

3–3.

We're all tied up — with one minute to go.

St. Croix are more desperate than ever. We haven't heard the "Lo-sers, Lo-sers" chant for a long time. The spectators are almost silent.

Dougan, trying to launch an attack on our goal, sends a long, high ball toward us. Holt gathers it and gets easily past Linh-Mai, leaving her sprawled on the ground after a desperate tackle attempt. Flyin' Brian rushes out and flings himself at Holt's feet, smothering the ball. Holt kicks at his fingers. Brian can't hold on. Holt scoops the ball over Brian and it arcs towards our empty goal.

I take in Flyin' Brian, sprawled helpless on the ground, one arm stretching toward the ball, fingers still hopelessly clutching for it. I glimpse Julie, her head and shoulders slumping forwards, her head sinking into her hands in despair. I see the Interchangeable Twins, for once not giggling, arms already around one another, comforting. I glimpse Shay and Steve, disappointment clouding their tired faces, but still alert. I even have time, extraordinarily, to see Conrad punching empty air in desperation, and Ma wailing a bad word. I see Mr. Walker biting his lip and turning to Miss Little, his arms out as if he's about to give her a comforting hug.

I see Mr. Sutton's fists clenched in frustration, and Miss Little — I can lip-read her in this fraction of a second — saying, "My poor children."

The St. Croix forwards are already turning away in celebration, arms up, looking towards the bleachers, where the old cry is starting again: "Lo-sers. Lo-sers."

Me?

I'm moving.

It may be in slow motion — but I'm moving.

There's no way I can reach the ball. I'm too big to be that fast. So I launch myself — my whole self — through the air, sticking one leg out in front of me. I reach the ball but my foot misses it. I try to pull back for another kick even as I tumble toward the ground. The ball hits my knee and goes up as I go down. It seems to hang in the air. I wish I'd hung in the air, too, so I wouldn't have this pain in my thigh where I land heavily in the mud. It seems as if the ball can't decide which way to go as it bounces from my knee — into our goal or away from it. We're all frozen, St. Croix as well as us. As the ball descends at last, Linh-Mai is struggling to her feet. She doesn't know where the ball is. It bounces off her head, knocking her back to the ground. The ball's in the air again. Julie is alert now. She reaches the ball before anyone else can move and heads it carefully down to Shay.

One second ago it was as if we were all frozen.

Now it's the opposite.

The St. Croix players scramble toward Shay. He keeps the ball, spinning around towards his own goal, then back towards the St. Croix end, eluding one lunging tackle after another. His head is high, surveying the field — and the spaces — before him, as he rolls the ball under his foot. Suddenly he sweeps it into an empty space on the right. The St. Croix defenders relax. They're tired, and they're not going to waste their energy chasing a ball going nowhere. They'll just let it roll out of play.

But Steve has been watching Shay; has seen his eyes sweep the field; can almost read his mind. Before Shay even releases the ball, Steve is running from the left side of the field to the right, into the waiting empty space. The St. Croix coach sees the danger and is screaming at his defence. The ball lands at Steve's feet just as the St. Croix defenders become aware of what's happening. They race to head him off, but he slips the ball to Nicholas, running forward and pointing ahead as he passes. Nicholas understands. As the St. Croix defenders turn on him, he pushes the ball through them and ahead of Steve, who lashes it into the top corner of the net.

It's 4–3 for us.

The referee blows the whistle to end the game.

Brunswick Valley are through to the next round. We're not Miss Little's Losers anymore.

13 THE PROUDEST MOMENT

How many more times am I going to have to go to the bathroom? This is the third time in the last hour. I'm so nervous I can't stop going, and we're not even at the game yet. In fact, we haven't even left Brunswick Valley School yet.

We're standing beside our team bus — or, in my case, running between the bus and the washroom — waiting for the twins, who are the last to arrive.

That's right — I said our team bus. Mr. Grant's company is paying for it — the bus, *and* new soccer uniforms for us all, *and* new cleats, *and* outfits for the cheerleaders, *and* a coach's track suit for Miss Little. The uniforms are blue, and the shirts have Brunswick Valley School on the front, and our team numbers and names on the back! The shirts have MAE, for Mr. Grant's company, Maritime Aquaculture Enterprises, on the arms. Steve's dad has suddenly turned into Miss Little's biggest fan. He wants Mr. Walker to send her away on coaching courses. After the game against St. Croix we heard him say to Mr. Walker, "It's just as I've always said. It doesn't matter whether the coach is a man or a woman. It's coaching *ability* that counts. I hope you understand what a jewel of a coach you have here, Mr. Walker, and I hope you'll do everything in your power to nurture and encourage her talent."

We just rolled our eyes.

We're like a real soccer team now. We're dressed like it, too, the boys in sports jackets and shirts and ties, the girls in dresses. They never wear dresses, except sometimes for school socials. We wouldn't know they had legs if they didn't play soccer. Julie's wearing a red dress and a short, white cardigan and looks more like a fairy princess than ever, except for the soccer boots. Shay can't stop gawking at her. "Shay, put your eyeballs back in," I say. He looks sharp in a navy blue jacket, white shirt, and his granddad's old soccer club tie. Shay whispered to me that his granddad had cried when he gave it to him to wear. Steve's wearing a black jacket, a black shirt, a dark red tie, and sunglasses. He looks like a gangster. Me? I've got grey slacks and a plaid blazer that Ma and Conrad gave me last night. I was clearing the dishes after supper when Ma told me to have the day off from my chores so we could go to the Second Time Around store to get my big game outfit. When we got back, Conrad gave me a tie he had borrowed from someone at work. It's green and has little soccer balls on it. I tried the stuff on.

"How do I look?" I asked.

Conrad grinned, winked, and replied, "You look just fine, big guy." Ma looked me up and down and said, "That's nice, lovey." Then she looked again and said, "That's *really* nice, lovey." I think I look good.

The reason for all this fuss is that we've been drawn to play against Shanklin Bay North School, the biggest of the big city schools. The game's in Shanklin Bay, a city on the east coast. It's a five-hour drive — in our special team bus — on the Trans-Canada Highway.

There are a bunch of supporters travelling with us: Shay's granddad, Mr. Walker, Steve's dad, Conrad, and Ma, as well as Ms. Watkins and some other teachers, plus lots of students and parents. They're all wearing something blue. Mr. Cunningham's here, too. He's talking to Miss Little. She asked him to have a coaching session with us when she heard we were drawn against Shanklin Bay. He showed us some ways we might try and close down the Shanklin Bay forwards, who he says have scored more goals than any other school in the province, and who are all tipped for places in the next Provincial summer games. He talked about angles and space, too. Shay and Brian and Steve understood. We tried. Brian's become a model student now. He hasn't been sent out of class for two weeks. Ms. Watkins keeps looking at him suspiciously, wondering what he's up to.

After the coaching session, Miss Little asked Mr.

Cunningham to be on the sidelines with her at Shanklin Bay, to help her.

Mr. Cunningham said to us, gruffly, "It's up to you. I gave up on you. That was wrong of me and I'm sorry. Maybe you want to give up on me."

We said he could come back if he promised not to explode.

He said he'd try.

The twins arrive. We hear them giggling before they even get out of their mom's minivan. Now we're all here.

"Let's get on board, everyone," Miss Little says.

Shay's granddad says, "One minute, please, Miss Little."

He nods to Conrad, who goes to the Sutton's Flowers van and gets a huge bouquet of flowers. He gives it to Miss Little. He gets a crumpled piece of paper from his pocket and reads, "This is from all the players and their parents, in appreciation of everything you've done for the team."

Everyone claps as Miss Little says, "Thank you, children. Thank you, parents." When she tells us to get on board again, we all stand back and make her get on first, and as she walks through the crowd we all applaud again. She smiles and sort of bites her lip. I see her chin trembling.

And off we go. We're chatty on the way, but the talking gradually stops as we approach Shanklin Bay, and as we drive into the city we grow more and more nervous. We gawk at the high buildings, which seem to be made mostly of pink and blue glass, and at the huge malls, which the Brunswick Valley mall could fit in ten times over, with Portage Street thrown in, too. We stare at the container ships in Shanklin Bay port, and at the oil refinery in the distance, with its burn-off flaring in the sky. It's Saturday afternoon and the streets are crowded with more people and traffic than we get in Brunswick Valley in a year. We fall silent as we approach the soccer field.

Our mouths drop open when we see it.

We're not playing at Shanklin Bay North School. We're playing on the Shanklin Bay Marauders' field, the city team that plays in the Maritime League. They let the school use their field for important games. We knew this — but we didn't know what it would be like. We're used to playing on our bumpy back field, surrounded by woods, with a scattering of people watching — sometimes. The Marauders' soccer field is not just a field. It's a whole stadium. We can't even see the field from outside. All we can see is a high fence surrounding it. We've never seen anything like it.

Our bus stops at the entrance, where people are lined up to get in. A crowd of cheerleaders rush out from the stadium and line up on each side of the bus door. They're wearing the Shanklin Bay colours of green and purple, and they're holding green and purple pompoms. As we get off the bus and file between them, they wave their pompoms and chant, "Brunswick Valley — welcome here. Come inside as we all cheer: Brunswick Valley — yeah!"

We feel like superstars.

We follow the Shanklin Bay cheerleaders to our dressing rooms. After changing into our new uniforms, we all go to the bathroom at least once. I don't know if I'm hot or cold because I'm sweating at the same time as my teeth are chattering. Shay says he's the same.

Miss Little and Mr. Cunningham are waiting for us outside our changing rooms. We follow them along a hallway and into a sort of tunnel. It's quite dim, but we see light ahead. We go up a ramp. We hear a band playing. Suddenly — whoa! We're in the biggest soccer stadium we've ever seen. We have to stop and take a breath before we can walk out into it. There are stands above and to each side of the tunnel and they're packed with spectators. There are still more people standing around the field and sitting in the bleachers on the other side. There must be more people here than there are in the whole of Brunswick Valley.

The band, in green and purple uniforms, marches off. We march onto the field to polite applause.

The grass is smooth and shiny green. It's cut to make stripes.

"Get your slippers on, guys," I say. "We're playing on a carpet."

The Proudest Moment

We kick a few soccer balls around to warm up, but mostly we just gawk. The Shanklin Bay North team are nowhere to be seen. We look for our supporters, and find them crowded into one corner of the stands. On the field in front of them, Natasha and her cheerleaders are finishing their routine. They've added twirls to the cartwheels and leg kicks and splits. We hear their voices faintly: "One — two — three — four. Brunswick Valley shoot to score! Five — six — seven — eight. Play BV and meet your fate!" Natasha had worked on that chant for a long time. As they finish, they turn and point to us. The crowd applauds politely again. We wave at Natasha and the others. They skip to the sideline. There's still no sign of our opposition.

Then, suddenly, smoke billows from each side of the tunnel, and just as I'm wondering when the fire department is going to arrive, the Shanklin Bay team trots through it onto the field.

Wow.

Do you know what a juggernaut is? We learned about it in school. It's an overpowering force that destroys everything that gets in its way.

That's what the Shanklin Bay team looks like coming through the artificial smoke. The stadium erupts in cheers and applause. The crowd stamps and claps and chants, "Out of our way — we're Shanklin Bay. Blow 'em away — Shanklin Bay."

At least it's not, "Lo-sers. Lo-sers."

The Shanklin Bay players, who all look twice as big as us, line up in front of their goal and take turns shooting. They kick the ball at about a hundred miles an hour. Then they line up on one side of the field and race across. They stop halfway and run the rest of the way backwards. They do stretching exercises, squatting on one leg and stretching the other one out as they press down on it with both hands.

Meanwhile their twenty cheerleaders dance and sing, "Shanklin Bay take the day. There's no doubt — you'll be OUT!" I guess 'you' means us — out of the Provincials. The cheerleaders strut backwards and forwards, swinging their pompoms. They do somersaults. To finish, they make a pyramid by standing on each other's shoulders. It's quite the performance — who needs a soccer game when you can watch this? — and we're not even bothering to pretend to warm up now. We're watching the cheerleaders, and when they jump down from the pyramid, doing more somersaults as they land, we applaud with the crowd, who are going crazy.

The referee appears on the touchline.

Miss Little waves to us and calls, "Gather round, children."

"Any last-minute advice?" Steve asks.

Miss Little turns to Mr. Cunningham and raises her eyebrows.

"I can't add anything to what I said the other day,"

he says. "It's your team. You got them this far. I could never have achieved that. You're the boss. Tell them what you always tell them."

The Shanklin Bay team is in a circle, their hands clasped together in the centre. The players roar their chant, their cheerleaders and supporters joining in: "Out of our way — we're Shanklin Bay. Blow 'em away — Shanklin Bay."

We look at one another nervously. Shay is biting his lip. Superstrike Steve is trotting in circles. Flyin' Brian is leaping at imaginary shots on goal. Julie is twiddling with her golden fairy-princess hair. I'm trembling so much I can feel my knees knocking together.

Miss Little beckons us closer.

"I have no last minute advice to give you, dears," she says, "I just want you to remember everything we've learned together, in kindergarten and on the soccer field. And now it's your turn to say your chant. Say it quietly with me."

We crowd close together and join hands: "Grace and dignity, dignity and grace; doesn't matter if you're top, nor who sets the pace. What matters most is not who wins, but how you run the race. So conduct yourself with dignity, dignity and grace."

We look at one another. Shay shakes hands with me. We're not sure why we do it. The Interchangeable Twins giggle. Flyin' Brian leaps for a final imaginary shot. Julie and Linh-Mai hug. Linh-Mai looks at Superstrike. He smiles. Linh-Mai whispers to Julie, "Steve smiled at me." Julie touches Shay lightly on the back of the hand.

Superstrike says, "Let's go, guys."

As we take the field with Shanklin Bay, the crowd roars. Amid the shouts of, "Out of our way — we're Shanklin Bay!" and "Blow 'em away — Shanklin Bay!" we hear our little band of supporters desperately trying to make themselves heard: "Brunswick Valley — all the way!"

I say to myself, "Whatever happens in the game, and whatever happens to all my friends and to me in the future, I'll always remember *now*. This is the proudest moment of my life."

ACKNOWLEDGEMENTS

Thanks to Margaret and Cayleih and the students of St. George Elementary School for responding to an early draft of *Miss Little's Losers,* to all at James Lorimer & Company for help and advice in developing it, and to Nancy, as always, for her patient support and perspicacious comments on outlines and drafts.

MORE SPORTS, MORE ACTION
www.lorimer.ca

CHECK OUT THESE OTHER SOCCER STORIES FROM LORIMER'S SPORTS STORIES SERIES:

Falling Star
by Robert Rayner

He's super-talented on the pitch, but lately Edison seems to have lost his nerve. He hesitates and misses shot after shot. Can a ragtag group of soccer misfits show him what the game is really about before it's too late?

Just for Kicks
by Robert Rayner

Toby's not the greatest or most athletic player on the field, but he sure loves to play. But when new coaches arrive and try to organize the pickup soccer players into a league, it doesn't matter who's friend, foe, or family — it only matters who wins.

Out of Sight
by Robert Rayner

Lately, the star goalkeeper on Linh-Mai's team has been acting a little strange — missing easy saves, passing to the wrong teammates, not noticing Linh-Mai's new glasses . . . Linh-Mai thinks he might need glasses of his own, but the problem may turn out to be more serious.

Total Offence
by Robert Rayner

Toby and Maddie absolutely love playing soccer, but they also love the food at Fat Vinnie's Family Diner — especially the delicious Chocofudge Super bars — and it shows. So when a tough new coach demands that they get fit or face getting cut from the team, they have to make a choice: do they tackle their waistlines, or get stuck on the sidelines?

Suspended
by Robert Rayner

There's a new principal at Brunswick Valley School, and the establishment is out to shut down the soccer team. For team captain Shay Sutton, the only way to fight fire is with fire, and he enlists the aid of two high school thugs to help them out.

Corner Kick
by Bill Swan

Michael Strike's the most popular guy in school and the most talented soccer player around. But then a new kid from Afghanistan arrives who can show him up on the field, and threatens to steal his spotlight . . .

Trading Goals
by Trevor Kew

Vicky lives for soccer, and dreams of being on the national team. But when she suddenly has to switch schools, she finds herself on the same team as her fiercest rival, a goalkeeper named Britney — and there's only room for one girl in the net.